Intrusions

Barbara Winkes

ISBN: 978-1-0693045-0-6

Cover art © May Dawney Designs

Created with Atticus

For D.

Chapter One

I t was a slow morning for Officer Kate McCarthy at the front desk, her mind wandering more than she would have liked. Perhaps this was the calm *after* the storm for all of them.

Time didn't heal any wounds. It was all about what you did with that time. She had raged and cried, grieved, questioned, and eventually picked up the pieces, and so had everyone around her.

Today, Jordan and Ellie would be back at work after their vacation. Kate was happy for their friends and their ability to deal with the aftermath of a traumatic situation. She could also admit she was jealous of them, just a little bit, because their relationship seemed so...urgent, unavoidable. She had wondered if that's what she and Jensen had been, and with each day passing, Kate felt more unsure and guilty about that question.

She was moving forward, if not moving on. It was much too early for that.

Moving into an apartment with Ellie had been a good idea, but she worried how long that could last.

Then there was Derek. She wasn't looking for a Happily Ever After. Especially not with another cop, after having seen how quickly those plans could be crossed out by a maniac with a gun.

Derek made her laugh, and that was something Kate needed most at this point in her life. She held on, even though there was talk behind her back. There had been talk about Jordan and Ellie too. Eventually, people moved on to the newest gossip.

"Here. If you need something to pass the time."

Libby sounded sympathetic as she put a tall latte in front of Kate. The front desk wasn't anyone's favorite, but every once in a while, it was your turn.

Libby had been there during the ambush, injured, one of the last people to see Jensen alive. Sometimes, Kate envied her friend for the latter, but she never said it out loud.

"Thanks. I guess a lot of people are still on vacation. It's pretty quiet around here."

"Yeah. Actually, I don't mind quiet for five minutes. Have you seen Ellie yet?"

"I picked them up last night. She should be here any moment. I don't think she wants to be late on the first day after vacation."

"No, that that's not like her," Libby agreed.

The door opened, and a middle-aged woman walked inside, looking tired and uncertain.

"At least it looks like I'll have some work after all," Kate commented.

"All right. See you later."

Kate nodded to her friend and turned her attention to the woman. "Good morning. How can I help you?"

"I...I hope this is the right place to do this, but I don't know what else to do." The woman's eyes were welling up. "I need to report my daughter missing. I know something happened to her."

"You're in the right place," Kate assured the woman, wondering why she had thought there might be any other place for a missing persons report. "When did you last see your daughter?"

"Last Thanksgiving."

Kate's disbelief must have shown because the woman hurried to explain. "She's in college in Iowa, and she doesn't have the money to come visit often, but we chat all the time. Well, at least we used to."

While Kate was sympathetic, she was also hopeful that this mother's worries could be eased soon. Away in college, kids did a lot of things their parents would not have imagined. It was only natural that their attachment would loosen with time and distance.

"I know what you're thinking, but something strange is going on. She sent this back."

She held up a bracelet for Kate to see. "It was her grandmother's. Not worth a lot, but she loved it and hardly ever took it off. I tried to talk to some of her friends on the phone. No one knows anything. It seems like she's just gone, but no one cares."

"Did you try to contact the local police?"

"I thought about it, but the reason I'm here is that Jennifer should have come home last night for her aunt's funeral. I last spoke to her when she left for the airport. She never arrived. Please, you have to help me find her."

"We will do everything we can," Kate said. "I need some more information from you, and we can talk to our colleagues in Iowa."

Perhaps this wasn't a simple story of a freshman testing her new freedom. In any case, Kate preferred helping others to trying to figure out her own life. She hoped Jennifer Beaumont's case wouldn't be quite so complicated.

∽∾∾

Jordan woke the same way she had in the past two weeks, her arms around Ellie, breathing in the scent of her skin. There was something wonderfully serene and perfect about this, even

3

on the occasions that nightmares had followed them into their sleep. Hers, Ellie's. It didn't matter in the long run, as long as the mornings started like this.

The only difference was that in the past two weeks, mornings hadn't started with an alarm and a ringing cell phone at the same time.

Since she was closer to the offending objects, Ellie turned off the alarm and picked up Jordan's cell phone.

"It's Kathryn," she said. "She left a message. Do you want to...?"

"No."

Of course, with the two of them being home for more than twenty-for hours, her birthmother felt the need to pick up her efforts to rekindle their relationship. Not that there was anything to rekindle, as far as Jordan was concerned. "Five more minutes," she whispered.

Ellie didn't protest, just laid down the phone and snuggled back into the place where she'd been before.

"We'll be late. I really wanted to get breakfast before work."

Jordan made a non-committal sound. Food didn't hold much of an appeal this early in the morning, and for sure, Ellie's naked body was a lot more tempting to her under any circumstances. Ellie had a point though.

Unable to stifle the smile, Jordan thought about waking up to an ocean breeze, making love before breakfast. Five minutes certainly weren't enough for that.

"We could have stayed at my place. It's closer."

"It's been a long time since I've had sex with someone when their roommate was only a room away."

Ellie laughed. "Come on, it's not like Kate is listening. You'll get used to it."

"Hm. Sure." Jordan knew that she didn't have a choice for the time being. After her abduction, Ellie had stayed with her for a while, but they had both agreed it was too early to talk about living together permanently. They both had made mistakes in relationships, getting involved too little or too much. This was different. This was for the long run, and so they were going to be cautious. It meant accepting the fact that Ellie now had a roommate who was dating Jordan's partner.

After two weeks in paradise, the honeymoon was over, time to go back to their everyday lives. It was the first time in probably a decade that she had taken this much time off, because she was passionate about her job—and frankly, there hadn't been much of a reason. Things between her and Bethany hadn't always been as bad as towards the end, but there was always something more important.

Escaping to Hawaii with Ellie couldn't have waited another day. She just wished it didn't end so soon. The unsolved questions they had left behind for a while were still here, waiting.

"Five minutes are up," Ellie reminded her gently.

"I hear you," she murmured and kissed her. Another five minutes passed before Ellie headed for the shower.

⁂

Ellie, too, regretted having to leave the bubble she'd been in with Jordan in the past two weeks. After their first vacation plans were rudely altered by a criminal breaking into her apartment and abducting her, she had been near paranoid. They'd changed the location, the airline and, against all odds, made it to Maui. Like Jordan, Ellie hadn't taken a real vacation in a long time, and she'd cherished every second of it. She was also happy to return to their circle of friends.

The first one she saw was Kate, at the front desk this morning. They hugged quickly.

"It's pretty busy here, but how about I make dinner later, and you can show me all the pictures to make me jealous?"

"That would be great. I've got to run now."

"Slept through the alarm?" Kate asked with a knowing smile.

"Yeah, something like that."

There wasn't much of a transition. A few minutes later she was on the way to answer a 911 call.

Marjorie Perkins greeted her in the doorway, casting a worried look at the house next door that appeared eerily silent now.

"A few minutes ago, there was a woman screaming, loud music, things breaking. I'm afraid someone's dead in there."

Let's not get ahead of ourselves. It wasn't how Ellie had hoped to start her workday. She knew from dispatch that a couple lived there, a man and a woman, no children. A couple of complaints earlier this year. There was at least one gun in the house.

Casey pulled up on the other side of the street, the backup Ellie had requested.

"Don't worry, Mrs. Perkins. We'll go check it out."

Marjorie Perkins snorted. "That's what the other cops said, but it never ends. How about you arrest them this time?"

"Would you please stay inside?"

"Yeah, sure, whatever."

She closed the door, but stayed behind the window, prompting a sigh from Casey. "Sometimes I think they're enjoying the show a bit too much, but in this case, she had reason to call. I've been here before. The woman seems okay, and they claim they're just partying, but something is off. How's the first day back?"

"It's like this." Ellie sighed. "What's their deal?"

"Apparently, the house was empty for a long time, so the owners decided to rent it out. That's what they got."

"Neat. Let's go take a look."

6

They walked over to the front door, and Ellie rang the bell, wondering why her heart was beating fast all of a sudden. Enough with the nightmares already—this had nothing to do with her personally. She had gone back to work as soon as she'd received a clean bill of health and then rescheduled her vacation with Jordan as soon as possible. Why the nerves, why now?

"Ellie. Everything okay?"

"Yes. Of course. I was—" She interrupted herself when the chain was removed on the other side, and a man opened the door just enough so they could see his face.

"What's the matter?"

"I'm Officer Harding, and this is Officer Lyons. We received a complaint."

"Sure you did." He made an exasperated sound but didn't open the door any further. "Are you hearing anything now? Of course not. I was working on something in the garage, and it was a little loud. It's in the middle of the week! Some people need to get a hobby."

"Someone mentioned screams," Ellie said. "Did you or anyone else hurt themselves? Your wife is home?"

"No and no. Is that all?"

Ellie realized that she was tempted to let it go, head back to her car and take the next call. Her mind was busy spitting out all kinds of worst-case scenarios, the man pulling a gun at any point, a horror scene inside...She was aware of Casey's surprised sideways look as the silence stretched on and cleared her throat. "Would you mind if we came in for a moment, took a look around?"

"You guys have a warrant?" he spat. "Didn't think so. Well, in that case, I do mind."

"A witness heard a woman scream. Since you say your wife isn't home, I'd like to know who that was. I can make the call right now and be back with a warrant, but if someone's hurt, it would help you if you let us help them."

"Fuck you," he said, but surprisingly yanked the door open. "Whatever. There's no one here."

Ellie stepped over the threshold, her throat tight and her heart hammering. Those weren't her instincts at work, just a whole lot of bad memories and imagination. Jonathan Darby. Josh Ward. One behind bars, one dead, but that didn't mean there weren't others like them.

Casey followed her inside while the tenant, George Delaney according to dispatch, stood with his arms folded across his chest.

"I do some carpentry from home, okay? I use a saw. It makes noise. There was no woman screaming."

"Could you show us the garage?" Casey asked after they had checked the surprisingly small inside of the house. There was no cellar or visible attic, two bedrooms, one bath, a kitchen that didn't look like much cooking was happening here. It was modest, but there was nothing to suggest a crime had happened here.

Ellie thought that if he had to clean up something, he had to have moved very fast. Feeling light-headed, she reached for the counter, steadying herself. Neither Casey not Delaney had noticed. He opened the door to the backyard for them, and they walked to the garage.

Instincts? Flashbacks? It wasn't fair, Ellie thought angrily. She was supposed to be better. Hawaii was supposed to have made everything better.

She wasn't sure if that was true anymore. In her first week as a rookie, she hadn't been this scared...then again, lots of bad things hadn't yet happened.

Chapter Two

T he first people Jordan met were Detectives Waters and Doss—he certainly had no interest in vacation tales, and Maria Doss cast her a somewhat jealous look. It was amusing. In the past, Jordan had barely noticed when colleagues returned to work with a tan, nor had she cared much. It seemed like everyone else found a way to slow down sometimes. She had been restless and antsy when off from work, and her deteriorating relationship with Bethany hadn't helped.

Things were different now, with Ellie. She settled behind her desk and went through phone messages and emails left in her absence. She received a text from Ellie, informing her that they'd have dinner at Ellie and Kate's apartment tonight, which made her smile. Even though the logistics could be a bit awkward, this was the best solution for the time being. Jordan was grateful Ellie understood that she needed that space, still, and it didn't mean she didn't want Ellie in her life.

The next time the phone rang, it was Derek.

"Apparently, Gerald Ashcroft has died. They called in the family doctor, and he notified the police. I'm on my way. See you there?"

"Wait. Where?"

"What, you don't know where the Ashcrofts live? I think your brain is still working on vacation time. Okay, write this down."

"Got it."

She was still wondering where Derek got the idea that she should be familiar with the place. Jordan had heard about the extremely wealthy family but never given much thought to where they lived. Before she could leave, the lieutenant emerged from his office and called her.

"You're leaving for the Ashcrofts?"

"Yeah. Anything I should know?"

"It would be best if you solved this case yesterday. There's a lot of pressure on this one, and the fact that the youngest son is the litigious kind, is the least of it. This family practically owns half of the city."

"Really? I wasn't aware of that."

"You are now, Carpenter. Tread carefully and make it quick."

"Did you give Henderson the same speech? No, don't answer that. I'll let you know as soon as we know more."

"I appreciate that," he said and went back to his office as Jordan left the department.

It was a half hour drive to the outskirts of the city to reach the sprawling Ashcroft estate. Uniformed officers guarded the gate, and she encountered another squad car on the driveway, before parking in front of an impressive mansion with huge marble pillars. Jordan couldn't help it, she stopped and stared for a moment. It was rare for her job, or in general, to be confronted with such luxury.

"Nice place, huh?" Derek had arrived as well. "I could imagine living here. Or driving that baby," he said with regard to the Ferrari parked in front of the building.

"Now's not the time. Someone died in this nice place. Let's do this?"

He laughed. "I thought two weeks in a tropical paradise would make you less cranky."

Jordan chose not to comment on his assessment.

"That's a lot of police presence here," she said instead. "Does anybody still think it was an accident? What happened?"

"He fell down the stairs," Derek explained. "By himself, or someone made it happen, we don't know yet."

"How old was he?"

"Seventy-two. In good shape."

They walked inside and into the grand entrance hall, a grand wooden staircase leading to the upper floors, a huge chandelier...The image was only marred by the body at the bottom of the stairs. Jordan noticed a man in his fifties and a slightly younger woman talking to uniformed officers.

Officer Libby Marshall noticed them and came over.

"Dr. Snyder, and the housekeeper, Mrs. Santos. She found him this morning when she went to get him after preparing breakfast. She called Dr. Snyder, and he called in the police."

"Okay, thanks. Let's find out why she called the doctor first," Jordan said to Derek. "If Ashcroft was alive when she found him, he might have been able to tell her something." They joined the small group and introduced themselves. Up close, she could see that Mrs. Santos' face was tear streaked. The doctor's gaze lingered a little too long on Jordan for her comfort.

She assumed he didn't consider her appropriately dressed to investigate the murder of a man this rich. Tough luck. He'd have to deal with her, while Derek carefully took the housekeeper aside.

"Dr. Snyder, you called the police earlier. Do you have any reason to believe someone could have harmed Mr. Ashcroft?"

He shrugged. "Not specifically, but I'd expect you to know that this is procedure in cases of sudden and unexpected death."

She would have loved to be back on the beach instead of being schooled on procedure by a good old boy.

"Yes, of course. I'd still like to hear your thoughts."

"He was a good man, decent to everyone. Someone of his standing will attract resentment over the years, jealousy mostly, but I don't think any of his adversaries would go as far as murder him. There's mutual respect in the business community, especially with men like Gerald who run an honest company."

"I see." Jordan kept her thoughts to herself. She doubted anyone could make this much money without angering people along the way, and regarding the mutual respect...*You wouldn't know anything about it*, the doctor's condescending gaze said. "What did Mrs. Santos say to you?"

He shrugged. "She was in a panic. I couldn't understand her at first. Finally, she managed to tell me that Gerald had fallen down the stairs, and that he needed a doctor."

"So, he was alive when she called you?"

"That's hard to tell. She was near hysterical at the time, in shock, and probably, denial. She has worked for him a long time—and he treats all his employees well."

Jordan cast a quick look over to where Derek was standing with Mrs. Santos. Fresh tears were running down her face. How close exactly had she been to her employer?

"As his doctor, can you tell me of any conditions that could have led to his fall?"

"Anyone can stumble, but Gerald was in good health. No prescription medication, he got his exercise in every day, ate well...This is either a tragic accident, or one of his no-good children wanted to inherit before it was time."

Jordan remembered the lieutenant's remark about the youngest son who was keen on lawsuits. "Why do you say that?"

"Well, Gerald wasn't just my patient, he was a friend. He told me things. Linwood is the only exception. He might be able to run the business and not run it into the ground. Abby and Craig, however...If they ever got their hands on that money, it's not going to last long."

"I'm sure Mr. Ashcroft left a will?"

"Yes, but you need to go through his law firm for that. Knowing Gerald, there could be a few surprises in there." For the first time since she'd met the man, he was showing emotion.

"I'm sorry for your loss," Jordan said. "We'll be in touch."

"You better. How much longer will you leave him here?"

"The crime scene techs will be done in a moment, don't worry. The coroner is already here."

"Pleasant," she said to Derek when he was finally out of earshot. "We have a number of suspects already...unless this poor man really fell down those stairs all by himself."

"Poor is not a word I'd use to describe him," Derek muttered. "As for the suspects, let me guess. The do-no-good kids. Apparently, they're not friendly with Mrs. Santos, and on the verge of being estranged from their father."

Jordan studied the dead man who was wearing PJs and a robe. She crouched down to take a closer look, careful not to get in the ME's way.

"Could be that he woke up from a noise, went to check it out, and someone...Mrs. Santos' room is where?"

"In another *wing*," Derek told her.

"Okay. If it happened very quickly, we could believe that she didn't hear anything."

"The head wound could be from the fall, but maybe someone hit him."

"Hm. Maybe." Most of the blood had been pooling beneath his head. Jordan tried to picture the scene on top of the stairs. If there was an attacker, had Ashcroft seen them—confronted them? Or had the perpetrator come up behind him?

"What's this?" she asked, pointing at a stain on the leg of the PJ bottoms. With a gloved hand, she drew the fabric aside carefully to expose the cut on Ashcroft's shin. There was a small smear of red on her glove.

"He cut himself, came down to find a bandage and stumbled?"

"No." She shook her head. "You can't tell me that his *en suite* isn't all stocked. We'll check in a second, but I don't think he would have to come down for that."

"It's a very clean, precise cut," the new ME, Melissa Adams, remarked.

"From around the same time he fell or was pushed down those stairs?"

"No spoilers," she said with a wink to Derek. "You'll have to wait for the autopsy. Speaking of which..."

"We're good, thanks," Jordan told her. She and Derek stepped onto the stairs.

"They're slippery," she noticed.

"Yes, but living in this house all his life, he would know."

Mrs. Santos had come up behind them as they were walking up. "Those stairs were recently redone," she explained. "Gerald...Mr. Ashcroft had ordered the carpet, but delivery was delayed."

"We will certainly look into that," Jordan assured her. When the housekeeper lingered, she added. "We'll be here a while. If you could please tell the staff we need to talk to all of them? We'll also have to take everyone's prints."

"Sure. You can use one of the conference rooms."

Jordan tried hard not to look too impressed, knowing she was probably failing. "We will also need the footage from any security cameras around the house."

"There aren't any."

Jordan had been slow to hide both her surprise and her frustration at this puzzling fact.

"We have the gate...Gerald always said we live in a paranoid world already, and he didn't want to add to that—and why would he? Everyone loved him...Excuse me," she said, turning away.

"Thank you for your help, Mrs. Santos," Jordan said softly. The housekeeper nodded and then went to talk to the staff.

"A cousin of mine worked here for a summer job, a long time ago," Derek surprised her when they were alone again on the first floor. "Are you saying you never followed any of the gossip about the Ashcrofts? Wow."

"It never really came up for me. Okay, show off. What do you know about this family?" Jordan asked. They had found the master suite where the bed was undisturbed.

"Linwood Ashcroft is the youngest, but he's supposed to take over business one day...I guess that day came sooner than expected now. Abby has gone into lots of different ventures, but as far as I know, none of them hit big, and then there's Craig, the oldest."

"What does he do?"

"I think he works as an accountant for Ashcroft, but there's something else...He was supposed to marry the daughter of one of Ashcroft's business partners, but then the wedding was canceled, and not much longer, he came out as gay."

"I'm impressed."

"That's all part of local history," Derek said. "I find it fascinating."

"I can see that." Jordan looked through the cabinets in the master bathroom, finding a bottle of Tylenol, a prescription drug that, upon a closer look, turned out to be sleeping pills—why hadn't the doctor mentioned it? Didn't he think they would find it?

"Let's get this to the lab," she said, bagging the bottle. "I'd like to know what exactly is in this. What else did you get from the housekeeper? Doc says she was too heartbroken to think clearly, that's why she called him first."

"Yep, her story matches. She says she was hoping he was only unconscious, but by the time Snyder arrived, she had to realize he was dead. According to her, Ashcroft was one of the best people who ever lived. Lots of charity work, always friendly to his employees."

"I get the feeling she appreciated him for more than his charitable work. Any ex-wives?"

Derek looked almost offended at that. "His wife died ten years ago. He never remarried. I want to look into the kids as soon as possible, if only to rule them out. It's creepy to think that your own kids could want you dead, isn't it?"

"Very," she agreed, and he made the connection a split-second later.

"Shit, I'm sorry. That's not how I meant it. You had no choice."

"I know. No offense taken." He was right, she'd had no choice other than to shoot TJ Pratt. He had survived and was currently serving a life sentence. Truth be told, Jordan didn't think of the man as her father. He was just someone her birthmother had slept with, unfortunately. "You're right, in any case, and now we need to let those kids know that their father died before the press gets wind of this. The lieutenant thought it was important to remind me, no mistakes."

"Mrs. Santos gave me the address." Derek looked unhappy, which Jordan could relate to. This was definitely the worst part of the job. However, there was a chance that one of them already knew.

There was no blood or anything out of order in the garage, just wooden planks in various sizes, paint, and tools. Ellie still felt uncomfortable in the small confines of the space, reminding her of other dark, small spaces.

"What else?" Delaney asked.

"This is what got you three complaints with your neighbors?"

"That bitch is nuts. They don't like us here, because we rent the place, so they're trying to make us leave."

"You have a license to run this business from home?"

Ellie scolded herself for not thinking about that question.

"Actually, yes," he told Casey. "Check that if you want. Hell, those people complained about the kindergarten on the other end of the block. They don't like any changes in the neighborhood."

"I'd still recommend you try to keep it down a bit with the music. Show some good will. You still have no idea about where they could have heard the screams?"

"Oh, for God's sake, call my wife at work and ask her if she's all right." He unlocked his cell phone and opened his address book.

"I don't think that's—"

"Why not?" Ellie interrupted Casey. "So we can wrap this up."

"Sure. Lil? It's me. The neighbors called the cops again, said that someone was screaming. Probably the saw, but you know how they are. A cop wants to talk to you, make sure I didn't cut you to pieces."

Ellie flinched. Delaney handed the phone to Casey. A few moments later, she gave it back. "All right, Mr. Delaney. Thanks for your cooperation."

"Next time, go next door, you might find something there. That lady keeps watching from behind her curtain all the time. Now that's creepy."

"That was weird," Ellie said once they were back on the sidewalk and on their way to the car. "I mean...I'm beginning to understand why Jordan likes to live in the middle of nowhere. I hope it will work better with my new neighbors."

"Some people just can't compromise," Casey suggested. "At some point, you got really pale in there. Are you sure you're okay?"

"Yes, I'm fine, don't worry."

It would be ridiculous for this to happen after she had already gone back to work, after that fantasy vacation. Ellie was determined to be fine. The mindset had carried her through some tough spots before, and after all, she wasn't alone anymore.

"He's dead? I can't believe it! Are you sure?"

Abigail Ashcroft's eyes filled with tears, imploring her visitors to take back their words. Unfortunately, that wasn't going to happen. People said the strangest things when confronted with the finality of death.

"I'm sorry," Jordan said. "Can you tell me when you last saw your father?"

"I don't know, two months ago?" Noticing the look Derek and Jordan exchanged, she hurried to continue, "I know what you're thinking, but it's not like that. We had a bit of a fight, but come on, I would never...I was going to give him a great chance to invest in an amazing business, but he wouldn't listen to me. Dad could be really stubborn about these things. I can't believe..." she said again and started to cry in earnest. "It must have been an accident, I can't imagine anything else. Everyone loved him. I can't think of anyone who wanted to do him harm."

"Do you know about any medication he might have been taking?"

Abby looked confused. "I'm not aware that he was taking any. Good genes, he always said. One can only hope. Oh God. What's going to happen now? Does Craig know? This is going to hit him hard."

Interesting, that she only mentioned one brother. "We will meet with your brother later. I understand that Linwood, your younger brother, is out of the country?"

She made a dismissive gesture. "Of course he is, at a time like this. He'd kill is own grandmother to make a dime...Wait, that's not how I meant it! It's just a figure of speech, okay? He can be a nuisance, but he wouldn't kill anyone."

"Craig was closer to your father?"

"Oh, yes. They had dinner every other week, discussing the books. Both of them have a passion for the boring details."

"Well, the boring details can make or break a business. Can you tell us about the business venture that you would have liked Mr. Ashcroft to invest in?"

Her eyes lit up. "You're really interested in that? I can show you. Come with me to my office." The invitation was mostly for Derek, as it seemed, but Jordan followed anyway, taking in the family pictures on the mantel. One picture of the whole family, including Abigail's late mother Sarah. There was a little girl with the same honey blonde hair, obviously Abigail's daughter. No man—or woman—in the picture. From the display, it wasn't hard to guess that she didn't get along with Linwood, Dr. Snyder's favorite, all that well. Had Ashcroft played favorites as well? Based on everything they heard so far, he had to have been a saint.

Abigail's house wasn't small, but nowhere near the extreme luxury of the Ashcroft mansion. She led them to an office with a view of the mountains in the distance. On the desk, there were scattered sketches. She picked up one of them.

"I came up with a great new concept for a Mascara brush. I know women will flock to that, but Dad just didn't have the same vision. There's real money to be made in the cosmetics industry."

Derek's gaze said it all. Jordan shrugged in his general direction, stifling a smile. *Sorry, I can't help you.*

"This looks...interesting," he said. "I assume you presented a business plan to him?"

"I wanted to discuss the idea first, before I invested too much time, but..." She sighed. "As you can see, it's all a moot point now. He didn't think it was interesting at all. Men, right?" That was directed at Jordan.

"Sure. Ms. Ashcroft, is it possible you could help us get in touch with your brother Linwood?"

"Me? We don't really talk. On the other hand, if I tried to call him, he would know it's a catastrophe. But I'm sorry, I don't have his current number."

"Just one more thing. Where were you last night?"

"Last night? I was here, working on my business proposal, after I put Savannah to bed. Really, you don't think...?"

"I'm sure you understand that we have to ask this question, even to family members."

She gave Derek a wry smile. "Well, I do watch TV sometimes. Other than my daughter, who only sleeps well when she sees the light in my office, I don't have much of an alibi. I hope that isn't bad."

"We'll let you know when your father's body will be released for the funeral," Derek told her. "Thank you for your time."

Chapter Three

O ver the course of the day, a portrait of the Ashcroft family emerged, the story differing slightly depending on the people they were asking. Craig, like his sister, was shocked to find out about his father's death. While Abigail seemed to float from one idea to another with little motivation to stick with one, Craig apparently didn't have much of a life outside managing his father's books. They seemed honest and genuine, very different from the picture Dr. Snyder had described.

Family was never without complications, Jordan thought with a sigh as she was sorting out her notes at her desk. They would see the lawyer tomorrow morning to get a clearer picture of Ashcroft's business persona, the people he dealt with, and who among them might have had an interest in harming him. If he was as kind and trusting as everyone said, it wasn't much of a stretch to think he would have let almost anyone in late at night. They also had spokespersons of his main charities on their list.

The lieutenant had buried himself in his office, fending off calls. When confronted with what they had so far, he'd grumbled at them to keep going.

It wasn't all that much yet, but they'd know more once the autopsy was done, and they could determine whether the fall had killed him.

"Here. I get the feeling this day is going to be much longer," Derek said, putting a latte and a muffin in front of her. "I found the number of Linwood Ashcroft's hotel, but he's not picking up."

"Thanks. Blueberry. You're a good partner."

"I know it can't beat cocktails on the beach, but it's something."

"Wow. That seems like forever ago."

"So, you had a good time?" he asked.

"The best. I was seriously considering not coming back." She noticed the small group of uniformed officers at the far end of the room, Casey, Libby, and Ellie who waved and smiled.

"How are things around here?"

"Good. Things are good."

Jordan decided that if he wanted to stay vague as to his relationship with Ellie's best friend, Kate McCarthy, she wasn't going to prod.

"I'm glad to hear that. We can all use some peace. Now, if we could manage to locate Linwood Ashcroft before he finds out the news from the press…"

"Well, the reason why you can't, might be that he's sitting in my office while you're idly drinking your coffee," Lieutenant Carroll commented. "I can tell you he's mad as hell. What part of 'tread carefully,' and 'get this done quick' did you not understand?"

Their colleagues discreetly turned their attention to their work, though Jordan was pretty sure they were all interested in this scene. Her phone rang, and she could see it was from the ME's office.

"I'm sorry, sir, I have to take that." Saved by the bell. The ME called to discuss preliminary findings. "I understand. Yes, we'll be there. Sir, we need to go."

"This is not over. We'll be lucky if Mr. Ashcroft doesn't sue."

"For what?" Derek protested. "We didn't do anything to give him a reason for that."

Seeing that the lieutenant was not in the mood to argue, and curious about the ME's findings, Jordan ended the conversation.

"Come on, let's go."

❦

"Obviously, we have to wait for the tox screen, but I believe there are some things you might find interesting," Dr. Adams began. "Mr. Ashcroft here was in excellent shape. If we are in that shape, at this age, we can all thank the Universe. Guy worked out, ate well, didn't smoke. I'd say he didn't drink much either. Why are you flinching?"

"Nothing. Go on."

"However, I believe the cause of death was cardiac arrest."

"He was taking sleeping pills. Could that have caused it?" Jordan asked.

"We'll have to look at the specific ingredients. There are studies that have linked a long-term use to a higher risk of a heart attack, especially in patients already afflicted with heart disease, but neither seems to have applied to Mr. Ashcroft. His heart was healthy—so we have to wait for those further results. They can cause sleepwalking though."

"You think this might be an accident?" Jordan couldn't believe it. That would be too easy.

Dr. Adams shook her head. "I might have, if it wasn't for this."

"The cut on his leg."

"Correct."

Jordan took another look. Something didn't fit...If Ashcroft had taken the sleeping aid, he probably wouldn't have heard the noise and left his bedroom. If he had forgotten about it, what had caused his heart to stop?

And the cut...They had searched the bedroom. There was no sharp edge anywhere, no nail sticking out in the luxury mansion that might have caused it—the cut was too clean anyway.

"Wait. The way it looks like, it was caused by something very sharp—like he ran into it. There was something on the stairs that tripped him."

"That would be my guess," Dr. Adams confirmed. "It doesn't look like anything he could have obtained in a fight, or that he could have done to himself accidentally."

"There was no fight. He wakes up, is in some distress—gets out of the bedroom. He tries to get downstairs, maybe even try to wake Mrs. Santos before he calls a doctor."

"Possible."

"But then whatever tripped him, did the rest. He took a header down the stairs."

"Now you just have to prove it," Adams said not without sympathy. "I would go back to the house and take another look at those stairs."

"Thanks for the tip," Jordan said, and to Derek, "First thing tomorrow morning."

<hr/>

"First day, we made it. Yay!"

Ellie greeted Jordan with a kiss, plates in hand. "You're just in time."

"Great. Can I help you with anything?"

Jordan sounded tired. Ellie thought it might not be the best of circumstances to bring up anything or everything that hadn't gone so well on the first day.

"No, everything is pretty much ready. Let me put these on the table, and I'll get you a glass of wine."

Ellie had been home for an hour or so. After a long hot shower and getting into comfortable clothes, her spirits had lifted, and she was ready to write off her earlier reaction as a glitch, something that wouldn't happen again. In any case, she had pushed through. It was nothing to worry about.

"I'm sorry you got yelled at," she said while pouring a glass for Jordan in the kitchen, where Kate was putting the finishing touches on a spaghetti sauce.

"On the first day," Kate said. "Ouch. Didn't you feel like getting right back on that plane?"

"Well, yeah, I did, but he was partly right. We should have taken care of the annoying sibling first, but...at least he's not suing yet. What else is new?"

"Kate's been telling me about a new pub they discovered," Ellie told her. "It's a bit further from the precinct, but okay to walk to, especially from here. We could check it out some other time."

The *Code 7*, run by retired cop Carl Roth, had been most convenient and frequented by many of their colleagues. It was where Ellie had fallen in love with Jordan and decided she would take that chance no matter what. It was where indecent acts had once happened in the ladies' room. Now, there were just ruins and a mountain of rubble where the charming building had once stood, and Ellie still couldn't bring herself to drive past it in the morning.

Roth's son had once tried out for the police academy but never made it past the first two weeks. Subsequently, while working in his father's bar, he had nurtured a resentment against its customers and one day decided it should all go up in flames...It hadn't been Danny Roth's plan A. He had paid a junkie to attack, and another time, abduct Ellie, hoping he could play the rescuer and be hailed as a hero. When that plan didn't work out, he proceeded to blow up the *Code 7*, the fact that no one had died in the explosion, his only saving grace.

The *Code 7* was gone forever. Now, Gerald Ashcroft was dead, an icon in the city for his charitable work.

She felt like getting back on that plane, too. Maybe they could both ask for a transfer. To Hawaii. Right.

"But that's for another time. Now, let's eat. I'm sure you never got to finish that muffin."

Jordan, too, was aware that there was a lot on her mind. At least they'd let it go for one evening.

"You're right about that. It was gone when I came back."

"Poor baby," Ellie said. "Lucky for us, Kate is a great cook. You'll love it."

After dinner, they finally got to watch vacation photos on Kate's flat screen TV. Only a couple of days away, those memories seemed unreal already. Why was it that the bad things always seemed to stick, and you had to fight so much harder to let go of them?

Jordan's ex, the FBI psychiatrist, might have an answer to that question, but Ellie would appreciate not seeing her around for a while to come.

Jordan stayed over. Everything was going according to plan. Having to find a new favorite hangout was really a minor detail, wasn't it?

⌘

Jordan hadn't slept in this apartment, in this room, often enough to block out all small sounds, like the key in the front door after they'd turned in for the night, or the voices speaking in a hushed tone. She knew who the voices belonged to, but it didn't really matter. With Ellie asleep beside her, she reflected on her day, the new case and its implications.

Every family had their skeletons in the closet. Ashcroft had donated to various causes, though he wasn't keen on spending money on his daughter's rather flaky ideas that never worked out. The atmosphere in Craig's office had been tense when they'd asked him how his father had reacted to his coming out—then again, Ashcroft must have come around, because one of his monthly checks went to a major LGBT rights organization.

In pictures, he always smiled, engaged with the camera, and if it was all an act, he should have won awards.

Eventually, she fell into a sleep that was surprisingly restful. Another day, another morning came much too soon. The bathroom door was locked, so she decided to make herself busy and get the coffee started.

The machine came to life with a soft purr, much unlike her own. Finally, the bathroom door opened, and a yawning Derek Henderson emerged, wearing nothing but a pair of boxers.

So that was who'd been hogging the hot water. Jordan remembered hearing the front doorbell last night, thinking this was a little more than what she wanted to see of her partner. Too early in the day, anyway.

"Would you mind putting on some pants?"

"Don't be a prude, Carpenter," he said good-naturedly and poured himself a cup of coffee. "Hey. That's not bad at all. Besides, you're not wearing any."

"So many offensive things in a couple of sentences."

"Children, behave." Kate walked inside, carrying a box of pastries, and someone's stomach grumbled. If asked, Jordan would have denied it was her.

"Oh, you made coffee, awesome." Ellie who had joined the group, kissed her, and they settled around the kitchen table.

This was...strange, Jordan reflected. Kate and Ellie were talking like this was no big deal, the four of them hanging out for breakfast. Was it? She cringed. Jordan liked her boundaries between work and home a little straighter. That's why she was living in a house away from the city in a quiet neighborhood. That's why she hadn't moved in with Ellie yet.

She and Derek had seen some bad situations together. They'd just never gotten this...private, except one night when she got drunk, and he came to pick her up. Yeah, like that hadn't been extremely private. The memory made her cringe even more. She had reason to get drunk that night, but still...

"Hey, earth to Jordan. We'll go straight to the lawyer from there? Maybe the lieutenant will be in a better mood if we bring him something."

"Sure. If I ever manage to get a hot shower around here."

"Come on," Ellie said. "It's early."

"Yeah. I want to stop at the doctor's again. I want to know if he knew about the sleeping pills."

"You think he lied to us?"

Before Jordan could answer, her cell phone began to vibrate on the table, and she quickly picked it up. "Sorry. It's possible, but why would he do that? He knew that we would find out."

I am so sorry if I'm bothering you, but all I know is that I have to keep trying. This might be my only chance, and I want to take it.

Jordan shook her head at the screen and tossed the phone back on the table. Like words could make any difference at this point. Kathryn still didn't understand that she didn't want anything to do with her.

"Maybe just hear her out once. That seems to be all she's asking...and then you can leave it behind you," Ellie said softly.

"No, thanks. I know how this would go. If I say yes to one thing, she'll ask for another, and before I know it, she'll be coming around for dinner."

"Would that be such a bad thing?"

"You have no idea. Can I take that shower now?"

She hated to see Ellie flinch, but she couldn't help it. Kathryn had already worn down her defenses, and Jordan didn't know how to deal with that fact. She had done what she could to save her from TJ Pratt, Kathryn's one time lover who had wanted both of them dead. She had brought her clothes to the hospital. As far as Jordan was concerned, they were more than even.

Jack and Pauline were her real parents. No words could change that. Or dinner.

Halfway through dressing, she acknowledged that she would have to apologize to Ellie. Jordan would have liked to pay her dues right away, but when she came out of the bathroom, only Derek was waiting for her. Fortunately, this time, he was wearing pants.

❦

The man storming into the station didn't mince words.

"I need you to find my wife. Something happened to her!"

Kate was already talking to him, trying to calm him down. Ellie spun around at the sound of the familiar voice.

"Mr. Delaney," she said.

"Officer. I need your help." His demeanor was a complete one-eighty from the day before. What did that mean?

"Of course. Tell me what happened. We were there when you talked to her yesterday?"

Kate shot her a surprised look but jotted down some notes.

"Yes, but she didn't come home from work. Her colleagues said she took the afternoon off, wanted to come home earlier. I went out to get some supplies, but she never came home. And there was this weird text message." He took out his cell phone and showed her.

I'm going out with some co-workers today, someone's birthday. I'll be late. Don't wait up for me. Lil

"Weird?"

"Weird because it wasn't anyone's birthday, and she said something else at work. I drove by there before I came here, trying to find her!"

"Okay, I understand. How long were you out?"

"A couple of hours maybe. Maybe she did come home, and someone took her? Or she was in a car accident? You can check those things, right?"

"We will check all of it, I promise. For now, I need you to think of the places where your wife might have gone, friends, family, anyone. Contact them. We will let you know as soon as we know more."

Part of her was still thinking of yesterday, his defensive behavior, the neighbor reporting a woman screaming. This was all too much to be a coincidence.

"Thank you, Officer Harding," he said. "I know I wasn't very patient yesterday, but it's the third time this bitch was reporting me for nothing. Nerves getting thin. I really appreciate your help."

Nerves getting thin...a woman screaming.

"That's our job. Let me make a few calls now, okay?"

Ellie wanted to talk to the neighbor again, but she couldn't reach her on the phone, so she decided to stop by. Marjorie Perkins seemed to be well informed as to what was going on in the neighborhood. She might have seen something that, in the best-case scenario, would help prove that Delaney wasn't involved in his wife's disappearance. Ellie wasn't yet sure if she'd be so lucky. She'd hate to find another man who hated a woman so much he became obsessed with her—wanted to hurt her. It wasn't always a stranger. Sometimes, it could be the guy you saw almost every day but never noticed.

Or the nice guy who just sold you a house.

Lillian Delaney hadn't returned when she parked on the curb in front of Mrs. Perkins' house later today. Perkins' car was in her carport, and she opened the door to Ellie right away.

"It's you again. I swear I didn't call you this time."

"Mr. Delaney called us. He's looking for his wife."

"Oh, good luck on that. Maybe she finally ran away with that hippie who kept coming around. Delaney got in a fist fight with him once."

"Really?"

"Oh, honey, the stories I could tell you. Why don't you come in? I just made cookies, and there's a fresh batch of coffee."

"I have a few questions indeed. I'm sorry I have to tell you no on the cookies. Do you know the name of Mrs. Delaney's friend?"

"No. I'm not interested in their affairs," Perkins said as she led Ellie into a small, cramped living room, where, despite Ellie's protest, she poured two cups of coffee.

"Did you see Mrs. Delaney come home from work yesterday?"

"Yes, of course. I have no idea how they can pay the rent. He hides out in that garage all the time—there's something creepy going on, I tell you. She comes home early all the time, and she can't make that much. They don't even have children to take care of."

"Do you remember when?" Ellie asked, finally getting a word in.

"Around three. I wonder if he buried her in that garage."

"Let's not get ahead of ourselves, okay? Did you see her go out again?"

"No, and he was definitely there. I heard them fighting again. Makes you wonder why some people get married, don't you think? Are you married, Officer?"

"No, I'm not. Let's go back to the Delaneys for a moment, please. You're sure that she came home and never left, and they were both in the house."

"Absolutely," Perkins insisted.

"All right, thank you. I might need you to come to the station for a statement."

"That wouldn't be a problem at all. I'd like to help. I normally don't approve of the type, slutty, you know what I mean, but I don't want her to get killed."

"Yeah, I know what you mean," Ellie said, trying not to let her resignation show. With neighbors like this, a person didn't need enemies. However, Perkins' observations were curious, and completely contradicted Delaney's statement. Wasn't he aware that Perkins was behind her window almost twenty-four/seven? He himself had mentioned it. Was there something that had made him so angry he didn't care any longer?

"Thank you. You've been a great help. We'll certainly look into all of that."

"I hope you don't find out he's some sort of serial murderer."

You and me both.

Back in the car, Ellie made a call to Kate at the front desk. "Is Delaney still around?"

"No, he just left, said that no one he called had seen Lillian. Why?"

"Well, the neighbor did see her, and she says Lillian never left the house after she returned from work. With the complaint yesterday and all...I have a strange feeling about this. The neighbor is a bit over the top, but she's alleging something might have happened to the wife. We should get a search warrant for the house and garage, to make sure."

"I'm on it," Kate promised. "I'll call you back."

"Thanks."

Ellie sat in the car for a moment longer, then exited, unsure what to do next. She walked around the house, standing by the fence. Where was Delaney? What would they find in the garage, and could they get the warrant based on the testimony of an obviously hostile neighbor?

"You're still here. You're sure you don't want a cookie?"

Marjorie Perkins' sudden appearance made her jump.

"No, thanks. I'm waiting on a call from a colleague."

Perkins followed her gaze to where they could see the garage through the rackety fence.

If Delaney was so handy, why hadn't he fixed that yet?

"Yeah, let's hope there aren't any bodies in there. The hippie also came around one time, and I didn't see him leave."

"All of this will be cleared up, I promise."

Ellie hoped it would be today.

Chapter Four

M s. Santos greeted them at the door, dressed in black, her expression somber. She cast un uncertain look at the two uniformed officers Jordan and Derek had brought with them.

"I assumed you'd be back," she said. "How can I help you?"

"This won't talk long," Jordan told her. "We'll just take a look around."

"I'll be in the kitchen. Let me know if you need me."

Jordan and Derek walked into the foyer where the blood had been cleaned away, and up the mahogany stairs.

"I wonder if you weren't making premature promises," he said. "This could take a while."

"That's why we brought reinforcements. We have to check the entire staircase...though I don't think whoever did this put what tripped Ashcroft on the bottom half. The fall had to be severe enough."

Jordan went up to the top of the stairs and crouched down, studying the first spindle on the left side. There was nothing she could detect, so she ran her fingers over the smooth wood. Nothing. She tried the second, then the third, until she found it: a tiny indentation in the varnish that went all around. She moved to the other side of the stair. The spindle on the right had the same indentation, as if something thin and sharp had been wound around it, leaving a barely visible mark in the varnish.

"They must have used some sort of cable or wire. Wow. That's pretty evil."

Derek didn't disagree. "I guess we need Ms. Santos after all. Remember she said the stairs were done recently? This looks fresh."

"Yeah, this definitely happened after the work was done here." She ran her finger once again over the mark on the left spindle. Jordan straightened and headed back down again, joining Ms. Santos in the kitchen area.

"You told us that the stairs were redone—can you tell us when the company was last in the house?"

"They finished the varnish on the banister two days ago. This is why we had to wait for the carpet. They told us it takes seventy-two hours to dry and harden completely. Now...I don't even know what to do about this. His children certainly don't care or talk to me about it."

"One more thing," Derek added. "Can you show us where tools for gardening or general maintenance are stored?"

"We don't do much of that ourselves. Gerald always hired a firm—he believed in supporting small businesses, but yes, there's a shed. Let me get the key."

Of course, that would have been too easy. The only wire they found was a piece of mesh. Santos wasn't kidding when she said they weren't doing that work themselves.

It was time to see the lawyer, and, Jordan realized, she would have to do some more research on razor-sharp trip wire.

⁂

There was not a hint of blemish on Ashcroft's reputation. Enemies?

The lawyer all but laughed in their faces. Tamara Lyndon was in her late forties. Her firm had worked with the Ashcrofts for over two decades, and apparently, he hadn't given them much to do other than the day-to-day work.

"You wouldn't expect a man like this to see past his privilege, but he was truly an exception," Lyndon said. "People couldn't get angry with him to save their lives."

"Well, someone did."

"I can't imagine who would do such a thing. His business partners...some of them thought it was silly he was giving away so much to charities. He had a big interest in civil rights. Others just set up some amounts so they avoid paying taxes, and they couldn't care less about the causes. His kids...There was some tension, but I believe they loved him."

"What kind of tension are you talking about?" Derek asked.

This was better, the two of them working, boundaries in place.

"For one, I'm sure you're aware he stopped giving money to Abby's projects. She doesn't even have bad ideas, but she never sees them through, and Gerald decided it was time for some tough love. Well, it only meant he wouldn't finance the latest idea. She's still living comfortably. He worked with Craig through his gambling problem. The air was clear between them. Linwood—he was going to take over the company some day."

"Isn't that unusual, him being the youngest?"

"Not at all. He has the knack for business. Abby and Craig both had their...issues with money, and I think they are both aware Linwood is the best choice. Craig will stay on in accounting, and Abby hopefully comes up with the real next best thing. I'm sorry I can't help you much."

"That's all right," Jordan assured her. "We're trying to get a complete picture."

"How can you be sure it wasn't a break-in?"

"Nothing was stolen, and it didn't look like anyone forced their way in. We assume that Mr. Ashcroft knew his murderer."

"It's so sad. He was a good man."

This seemed to be the only thing everyone agreed on. That, and it was curious that no one had mentioned Craig's gambling problem before.

⁂

When they were back at the station, the lieutenant asked Derek for an update while Jordan went to see Dr. Adams.

"So, you escaped from another stern conversation upstairs," the medical examiner remarked. "Your partner wasn't so lucky?"

"I know you prefer to see him down here, but I'm afraid you'll have to do with me. What more can you tell me about Mr. Ashcroft?"

"We know he took a bad fall down those stairs, but the stuff he had in his system didn't help."

"The sleeping pills."

"No, that's the thing. The pills in the bottle were prescription medication but not sleeping pills. Digoxin is used to treat heart conditions, sometimes heart failure that cannot be controlled by any other medicine. One possible adverse side effect is ventricular tachycardia which can lead to sudden cardiac arrest."

"This drug alone could have killed him?"

"Yes. Someone wanted to make sure, huh?"

Jordan took a look at the cut on Ashcroft's leg. This had to have been planned a while ago, from the inside, by someone who knew a lot about Ashcroft's life, the staircase remodeling, the sleeping pills he was taking. Yet, everyone in that circle claimed they loved him.

"Can you pinpoint the time of death?"

"I'm so glad you asked. This kind of drug takes a while to take effect, and based on this, and the injuries...I'd say between two and four a.m."

"Okay." Jordan pictured Ashcroft taking the pill, not knowing it wasn't the harmless sleeping aid prescribed to him. He might have gone to bed, not feeling well and got up to go downstairs, maybe dizzy already...and there was the wire on the stairs.

For all the planning, the perpetrator had been suspiciously bad at covering their tracks. It was almost as if after the fact, they didn't care...or felt remorse and wanted to be caught.

"Okay, you're not going to question my expertise?"

"I wouldn't dare. Don't hit on Derek. He has a girlfriend."

"Easy, I'm just enjoying the view."

"All right then. Is that all?"

"Did you find anything about the wire?"

"Not yet. I doubt it's a special brand."

"One thing's for sure. Whoever did this, really wanted him dead. Even if the pills didn't do it, at some point he would have walked into that trap."

It was a chilling thing to think about, the safety of home compromised like this. Jordan thought she might have to do a paranoid sweep of her own once she got back.

⁂

Dr. Snyder was perplexed when they asked him about the sleeping pills. At this point, they didn't see it fit to share details about the heart medication that obviously hadn't been prescribed to Ashcroft.

"I told you, there was always trouble with those kids one way or another, but if Gerald had trouble sleeping, he would have told me. I'm sorry, I can't help you."

"Thank you, Dr. Snyder."

When they were outside the office, Derek continued, "What if Ashcroft was sicker than anyone thought? Maybe he asked for a second opinion, was recently diagnosed?"

"Yeah, maybe. Or someone knew very well what they were doing. Who had access to this information and Ashcroft's medicine cabinet? Who did he trust most?"

Derek shook his head. "I know what you're thinking, but Santos isn't the one. She had a huge crush on Ashcroft, obviously..."

"He didn't return the sentiment?"

"No. I can see where she would have had the opportunity to pull this off, but I wonder if the doctor and his patient have always been such good friends, as he says?"

"Good question," Jordan said.

Perkins didn't seem to have anywhere to be, and she had a lot to say about her neighbors too. Ellie was beginning to think that either the complete story was true, that Lillian had cheated on her husband, and he killed her in revenge, or that Marjorie had created a whole mystery in her mind. The truth was certainly more complex. As she listened to Perkins talking, Ellie heard a noise, a bump that came from somewhere behind her. She turned around, but there was no one, just Perkins' house.

"Do you hear that?" Ellie had meant it to be a rhetorical question.

"Hear what?"

There it was again, a repeated thump against wood. It seemed to come from beneath the wooden trap door of Perkins' cellar.

"Mrs. Perkins, would you open the door?"

"Why? I'm sure it's just some animal. I'll take care of that later, don't worry."

"Mrs. Perkins. Now."

The woman looked nervous, which had Ellie imagining a whole other story now.

"I don't have to, right? You can't make me without a warrant. That's what you were waiting for, right, to get permission to go into George's garage? Why don't you work on that? The bodies you might find..."

"You are acting suspicious. I'll have to ask you again."

"Okay, okay," Perkins muttered. "It's true what they say, you can't trust the police, they are always going for the wrong ones. The neighborhood was in order once, quiet, until they moved in. The Delaneys are the ones you should arrest."

She bent to turn the key in the lock, her elbow hitting Ellie in the chest the next moment.

"No, that didn't help at all," Ellie gasped before she got to her feet and ran after the woman.

Casey arrived the moment she put cuffs on Mrs. Perkins who let loose a stream of obscenities.

"Oh please, just take care of her," Ellie said. "I believe we don't need that warrant anymore."

"You okay?"

"Sure." She went back to the trap door and opened it all the way, revealing the woman trapped in the small space of the storage unit.

"Mrs. Delaney?"

"Oh, thank God! I knew she was a terrible person, but this was rich even for her."

Ellie reached down to help her climb outside. Other than a bit of dirt on her clothes, Lillian Delaney seemed unharmed.

"How did this happen?"

"She's been on our case ever since we moved in. Complained about everything, George's business, the music, hell, the flowers we planted in the front. If she could have called the police about that, she would have! When I came home from work yesterday, George wasn't there. Perkins came out, all friendly all of a sudden, and offered to bury the hatchet. I should have been suspicious. She had cookies and coffee all ready, and then she said she wanted to give us a bottle of wine from her cellar. I followed her downstairs. Stupid, right? She locked me in there. At least there was water and some food. I have no idea what her plans were in the long run, but they weren't good."

"I agree. I'm glad we found you. Let's notify your husband now. He's been looking for you all day."

Lillian gave her a wry smile. "Only today? You'd think your husband would notice if you didn't come home the first night."

"She sent him a text from your cell. You left your bag upstairs?"

"I can't believe this. Thank you." Spontaneously and unexpected, Lillian Delaney hugged Ellie. "I hope you're going to lock her up instead."

<hr>

"I didn't tell you about the gambling, because it has nothing to do with your case," Craig Ashcroft said, seeming indignant that someone might think otherwise. "I think it's outrageous that you keep bothering us in this time of grief. We are trying to plan a funeral. Linwood might hardly be right about anything, but he's right about this."

"Why not mention it? You must have expected us to find out at some point."

"It's not something I like to talk about, okay? Dad and I talked it over. I had therapy. That's it. I haven't touched any sort of gambling in over five years. If you'll excuse me now? I have to work."

Back at the station, they found that Ellie had a more successful day, having found a missing woman, and arrested the culprit, a neighbor with a lot of time on their hands and a penchant for drama and mystery.

"I'm glad you had a good day," Jordan told her. "I swear, the lieutenant gives me the evil eye every time we're back here without an arrest. At least, no one's suing so far, and...I'm sorry. For yelling at you this morning," she clarified when Ellie gave her a surprised look. "I know you mean well. I just want her to stop, and she's not listening."

"That's okay. Maybe you're right. Wait it out, she might give up at some point." Ellie didn't seem much convinced, but at least she had accepted Jordan's apology. The day was looking up. "I'll see you later at the *Night Shift*?"

"That name will cause some misunderstandings in the future," Jordan said with a smile. "Sure."

She and Derek spent the rest of the day talking to heads of charities Ashcroft had worked with. Interestingly enough, he supported LGBT rights, women in business and organizations helping individuals with various addictions. There was also a fund Tamara Lyndon had mentioned, assisting underprivileged children access sports and arts programs.

Jordan had dreamed about winning the lottery a time or two, but the reality of what could be done with that kind of money blew her mind. It wasn't surprising that most of the people she talked to were shell-shocked about Ashcroft's death—whoever wanted to do him harm, still a mystery.

Linwood had come around and wasn't talking about suing the department anymore, but he too had urged them to release his father's body so they could arrange the funeral. At this point, they didn't have much to argue with...but there was still the heart medication that apparently wasn't his.

She and Derek parted ways at the end of her shift before she joined Ellie at the new bar, the *Night Shift*.

It was bigger than the *Code 7* had been, the lighting a bit brighter. It would take some time getting used to another place, though it was a small inconvenience considering the kind of catastrophe they'd almost faced. She was glad to see Ellie alone at a table.

"Hey," she said, slipping into the booth, sharing a quick kiss with her. "So, this is the new hangout."

"I guess so. It's still crazy to think of what happened...He was among cops all the time, and no one suspected a thing."

"Sometimes it's the quiet, polite ones." Jonathan Darby had been polite, too, until she got to know him better.

"Yeah." Ellie sighed. "At least it's over now. Like the vacation. That was so quick, like a dream." She leaned into Jordan, and Jordan suspected that she had more to say, but silence ensued.

"You found that woman today."

"I was lucky. I guess she was too. What a bizarre way to handle a conflict with a neighbor, locking them in your cellar. I've had enough of those dark spaces. I think I might be getting claustrophobic or something."

"It will be better with time," Jordan said.

"We didn't really talk about...all of this," Ellie remarked. "Darby, Ward. Should we have talked more?"

"As far as I'm concerned, I'm not willing to give either of them any more space in our lives. Besides, the vacation was highly therapeutic even when we didn't talk." Her plan worked. Ellie smiled at the implication.

"No kidding. You feel like some more relaxing time tonight? You'll see, you're going to love being so close to work."

"Yeah, as long as Henderson doesn't keep stealing the hot water. You didn't want to christen the restroom here?"

She laughed when Ellie's eyes widened, as if she believed Jordan was serious about the idea.

"Got you there."

"Come on, I didn't think you were serious."

"You so did. No, it's all right, I like not being desperate for a place to spend some time with you...though that time was pretty amazing."

"Yes, it was. And we might want to change the subject right now."

"Go on. We're used to that kind of thing from you two," Kate said, pulling herself a chair. Henderson was stifling a grin, but wisely keeping his thoughts to himself.

After a waitress had taken their orders, Kate brought the subject of conversation back to work. "It's strange, two people reported missing in two days. You were luckier than I was. It turns out my girl got on the plane like her mother said and arrived on time. She rented a car and that's where we lose her. No sign of the car either, and there's the bracelet she sent back. Strange."

Jordan realized that the subject of a woman missing still caused her stress, bringing unwanted memories with it, Ellie's abduction, Darby's obsession with her that almost turned deadly. It was true, they had tried not to let these experiences intrude on their off-time, but sometimes, it was hard to keep them from bubbling up.

The Ashcroft case was so different, and yet mysterious. She felt a little guilty for being relieved about a case that, for once, was in no way personal. Of course they hadn't always been. With Darby haunting the town, her biological father turning out to be a career criminal, and the quiet polite son behind the counter planning and executing Ellie's abduction, they'd had more than their share.

If she could keep Kathryn from calling her, everything would be perfect. Right?

Jordan and Ellie were first to leave, and that night, Jordan was too occupied to listen to sounds from the hallway or the room next door. If anything, it was Ellie who might get them into trouble.

"Shh," she whispered, uncertain whether or not Ellie was making an honest effort. The appreciative sounds were both flattering and arousing, so Jordan didn't make much more of an effort to tell her to be quiet.

She moved up to lie next to Ellie who settled into her arms with a sated sigh, and this time, the silence was comfortable.

Kate and Derek had gone out for breakfast, so Jordan and Ellie had the place to themselves the next morning. Ellie told herself she hadn't made tiny backwards steps during the Delaney case. She was still dealing and moving on meanwhile. Life was good. She knew that Jordan's birthmother trying to force contact with her daughter was an issue Jordan still had to solve but compared to the life-or-death situations they had faced in the past months, it seemed...manageable.

If Kathryn didn't give up, that meant she was serious about wanting to change. In Ellie's opinion, this was the best-case scenario. If she gave up, like before, that would only prove Jordan's point. It would be sad, but she was still surrounded by people who cared for her and would help her cope. It wasn't like Jordan had too high expectations of her birthparents.

Today was the day Ashcroft's will would be revealed. Maybe that would help her catch a break with the case as well.

Chapter Five

"As I can see you are leading comfortable lives unlike so many others who suffer due to no fault of their own, I'm sure you will understand. I hope you remember that in the long run, we need to take care of more than just our own family. I wish for you to continue that legacy."

By the time Lyndon was finished reading, Linwood Ashcroft's expression had turned from a smile into an unreadable mask, Craig's face had reddened, and Abby was crying even harder.

Mrs. Santos was quiet, though she didn't look surprised.

The majority of the Ashcroft wealth was going to various charities. Linwood, Craig and Abby got $300,000 each, and Mrs. Santos $100,000 and selected pieces of jewelry and furniture. There was a college fund for Savannah, Abby's daughter, and the siblings were supposed to divide the rest of the furniture and assets between them. Ashcroft wanted the house to be turned into a modern therapy center benefiting victims of rape, domestic violence, and bullying and harassment.

The silence was explosive.

"Well, this is not completely unexpected," Linwood said.

"What the hell?" Abby sniffled. "Family is everything! What was wrong with him?"

"Maybe he realized that most of his family was trying to rip him off." Linwood again.

Jordan studied the exchange between the siblings with interest. Abby had invited her in, but she seemed to regret her decision now. Linwood was gloating. Jordan couldn't help but feel a certain kinship with Ashcroft—sometimes, it was better to invest in people other than your blood relatives.

For a man who had lived such a privileged life, he was surprisingly aware of the less fortunate around him. Maybe he'd just been tired of their pretense—and it was remarkable that all of them got the same amount. It might not seem much to them, but she'd seen lots of antique furniture in the Ashcroft mansion. They would not be broke and starving anytime soon.

"You know that's not true," Craig answered his brother. "We're all hurt, but let's not accuse one another. It's bad enough as it is, but here we are. It looks like we're all in the same boat."

"Oh, no, we're not. I didn't need to be creative with the books to finance my addiction—or some stupid idea that would never go anywhere."

"See, that's how it always goes. Maybe he couldn't stand Linnie's self-righteousness anymore."

Judging from the stormy look on his face, Linwood didn't approve of the accusation or the nickname. He composed himself.

"There is no mention of the fishing cabin. I wonder if he forgot about it? That's unlikely, after all he went just last month, all of a sudden."

Tamara looked puzzled. "That's right, not a word. I guess you'll have to go up and see what's there."

"I think it should remain in the family," Linwood said. "Since my siblings won't be able to, I'll take care of it. I'll go this weekend. Unless you need me to stay in town, Detective?"

"That's all right, Mr. Ashcroft."

"Wonderful. Are we done now? I need to get back to work."

Abby shook her head. Craig didn't say anything, but his expression spoke volumes.

"Perfect. The sooner we can all go back to normal, the better."

"Linwood, wait. There's more," Tamara Lyndon said. "We have to talk about the company, of course."

"Yeah, so? I know Dad wanted me to take over. Craig can continue to do the books, but I'll have someone make sure it's all legit."

"No, that's not what it says. I believe he must have made some changes recently...Gerald wants you all to be equally involved in the company. That means you'd need to take more responsibility, Craig. Abby, he wants you in marketing, but still as a voting member on the board."

"What the—?"

Jordan noticed with interest that this news got a rise out of Linwood Ashcroft.

No one had expected this.

The more she learned about Gerald Ashcroft, the more she liked him. He was giving them quite a puzzle.

꧁꧂

The waitress had directed Ellie to a table in the bistro where she was supposed to meet Jordan for lunch. Jordan had told her she might be late, depending on how her morning went.

Ellie had a lot on her mind—the case Kate had told her about, the Ashcroft mystery they were all trying to solve, her own reaction to dark, narrow spaces. At least, she hadn't been confronted with any since she helped Mrs. Delaney out of the cellar. That neighborly feud was over now.

At first, she didn't recognize the woman who had come in and headed straight for her table. Ellie thought she must be mistaken, but then she recognized Kathryn. Compared to the last time she'd seen her, in the hospital, after her ex-lover, Jordan's biological father, had tried to kill her, Kathryn looked surprisingly put together. Ellie perpetually imagined her younger, her and her husband Jim, a couple of irresponsible kids who had no idea how to take care of a child.

"It's Ellie, right?"

"Yes, but...Jordan will be here in a moment. I'm sorry, I don't think she'd appreciate us talking."

"I know. I need a moment of your time. I'm sorry about what I said in the hospital." To Ellie's dismay, she pulled herself a chair. "I know you care about Jordan, and that's why I need you to hear me out. I know she doesn't want to talk to me. I understand why, I really do, but I was hoping you could..."

"Convince her otherwise? I'm not sure I can do that. You've only reconnected..." Ellie couldn't help cringing at the word, and she thought maybe Kathryn did too.

"Recently. You have to give her time, and texting and calling all the time is not helping, I'm afraid."

Kathryn sighed. "Look at me. I don't have that much time."

"What do you mean?"

"Are you really interested?"

"She might be, but I am not. Leave." They both flinched at the icy tone of Jordan's voice. "You heard me."

"Jordan, if you want me to leave you two alone for a moment and—" Get this over with. Ellie didn't say it out loud.

"No, thanks. Kathryn?"

"Why won't you talk to me? How many times do I need to apologize?"

"Until you mean it. Have a nice day. And if you don't leave right now, I swear, I'm going to arrest you."

"Jordan," Ellie said quietly.

There were people at other tables looking on with interest.

Kathryn got up, her head down.

"You know where to find me," she said and left. Ellie was both relieved and worried as she watched her leave the restaurant. She and her husband had done something terrible, possibly unforgivable, but there was something about her Ellie found hard to ignore. Broken. There was no doubt she had suffered too. Ellie was anxious that even acknowledging this might make Jordan believe she was any less on her side.

"What the hell was that?"

Ellie couldn't answer right away because the waitress arrived at this moment.

"I really want that cheesecake now," Jordan mused. "And to think that Darla is the pregnant one..."

"Did you hear from her? How is she doing?"

"Don't try to change the subject. What was she doing here? Why are you talking to her? Don't ever do that again."

"I don't know, and I had no choice. It would have been a bit weird not to say a word. Look. I think it could be good for both of you. Just talk, that doesn't mean you have to forgive her or your father for anything."

"Jack is my father, not any of the men who had sex with her. It's unfortunate that they were involved in a case, but it's over now, and I don't need any of them in my life. I need *you* to not encourage them. I don't expect you to understand, but please, do as I say, that's all I'm asking. Where's that food now?"

Ellie understood a lot more than Jordan thought about the many issues simmering under the surface of this conversation. She had irrationally felt let down by her parents after their deaths, and she knew, in Jordan's case, there was nothing irrational about the sentiment. It seemed logical though, that talking to Kathryn would help all of them move on.

She was tired too.

"Yeah, I hope it will be here soon. I need to get back in a bit."

"I'm sorry."

"I know. It's okay."

Jordan took her at her word, and they changed to easier subjects. Work was always one of them.

⁂

"What happened? Did you see a ghost?" Derek asked when Jordan, back at her desk, tossed her jacket over her chair.

"Something like that. She's definitely haunting me," she muttered. "All right. I wish we could take a look at that cabin. Something tells me he wasn't up there alone, and that this did have something to do with Ashcroft changing his will."

"I agree, but we'll never get that warrant," Derek pointed out. "It's now in the siblings' possession, and I don't think they'll just let us walk in."

"Maybe they will. Abby might be open to the idea. I'll call so one of them can come sign the paperwork to release the body."

"Yeah, you do that."

Jordan was about to make the call when Linwood Ashcroft walked in, heading for her desk.

"Detective Carpenter," he said. "I apologize for the chaos earlier. I'm used to it from my siblings...but let's just say, this was quite the change of plans from Dad's point of view."

"It's good you're here. I need you to sign some forms, and then we'll be able to release the body."

"Yes, sure, thank you." Jordan caught Derek's speculative gaze. All of a sudden, the younger Ashcroft son didn't seem in that much of a hurry, a very different picture from the man who had threatened to sue the whole department only days ago.

"I was thinking that maybe you'd like to join me up at the cabin. I don't know, there might be something relevant after all. I know we're all wondering about the sleeping pills found at Dad's house. Maybe we'll find an answer as to why he was taking them."

"That would be helpful, thank you. I'll go," Jordan said, remembering Derek had mentioned he and McCarthy had plans for the weekend. Keeping her distance wasn't such a bad idea until she had figured out how to make it up to Ellie for her earlier outburst.

She wondered if there was a lesson in being confronted with these privileged kids who couldn't seem to let go and bring everything in their lives back to their deceased father.

He had made an honest effort, which was a lot more than she could say about her birthparents. Still, she was beginning to question if her anger towards Jim and Kathryn still served her. There was someone who could possibly help her with this answer.

She stole into her office for a few minutes to make an appointment, and Dr. Burns agreed to see her after her shift.

∞

"I haven't seen you in a while," Dr. Burns remarked.

Stating the obvious, Jordan thought. She made sure to attend mandatory appointments after the confrontations with Darby, Pratt. Experiences lingered, that was normal. Jordan could see the benefit in these conversations, but she remained wary. A long-term relationship with a psychiatrist had taught her that.

"I was pretty busy. I finally took a vacation which was...amazing. I almost forgot that normal people do that every once in a while."

"I'm glad to hear that. So, things are calming down for you."

"As much as they ever can, but...lately, I don't know. I've been yelling at people for no reason. I don't like to be that person."

"Have you been sleeping?"

"On and off." That was nothing new either. For all her griping about a person next door, she slept surprisingly well at Ellie's apartment. It didn't mean she had any less need for space. It simply meant Ellie was good for her. She'd better not screw this up. Jordan had high hopes since the vacation had gone so well, but she was disappointed in herself. And Kathryn. Come to think of it, none of it was so new. "It has nothing to do with a case, present or past, at least I don't think so. My birthmother wants to keep in touch...I really don't want to, and she can't or doesn't want to get the message."

"Have you thought about taking legal action?"

Jordan shrugged. "Not worth the time. She's not dangerous, just...persistent."

"What do you think would happen if you talked to her? Would that make the situation better or worse?"

Jordan gave this question some consideration. "Frankly, I don't know. I guess there's only one way to find out."

"It doesn't mean you're giving in or even changing your mind. Like you said, this is different from a case, though...I understand there is a connection."

"Yeah, but Pratt is not trying to reach me. In fact, I think we both would be fine if we never saw each other again. Darby has been quiet. *I* overreacted when I went to see him. It turns out he had nothing to do with Officer Harding's abduction. We're doing okay. I just need Kathryn out of my life again."

There had been a time when Darby wasn't quiet, in her mind, at least, but Jordan had worked hard to reclaim that space. It wasn't anything she wanted to touch right now, and Dr. Burns fortunately understood that.

Ironic that she couldn't seem to figure out what to do about Kathryn, given the other challenges in her life.

"What if you chose the terms? The place, the time you're willing to give her—it would give you more control than you feel you're having right now, and if she's genuine, she will probably agree. It's not a binding contract."

"I'm scared." Where the hell did that come from?

"What scares you?"

"Excuse me, there's somewhere I need to go right now. Thank you for your time, that was very helpful. I'll think about what you said."

"Are you sure you want to end this here?" Dr. Burns asked, sounding concerned.

"Yes, don't worry. I figured out something important."

On her way, Jordan stopped by the flower store. When Ellie opened the door to her forty minutes later, her eyes widening at the bouquet of red roses, she wasted no time.

Their passionate kiss had witnesses, and a moment later, Ellie stepped back, a blush to her cheeks. "I didn't forget Valentine's Day? Or an anniversary?"

"No. Why are you always around?" Jordan directed at her partner who was helping Kate into her coat with a smirk.

"Don't worry, guys," Kate said. "We won't be around for much longer. Thank you, by the way, for going up to the cabin, so Derek doesn't have to. We owe you."

"You certainly do. Have fun."

"Same to you," Derek said. "I see you're already forgiven. Smooth."

"Yeah. Now get out of here."

Jordan cringed at her own words, reminding it was the second time she had used them today in a scenario where they were uncalled for.

"Already gone. I'll see you on Monday."

Ellie regarded her curiously. "I better get a vase for these. They're beautiful. You already apologized though."

"Yeah." Jordan followed her into the kitchen. "I thought you deserved a bit more than sorry, considering that I'll leave you alone this weekend."

"Hm. How sorry are you?"

"Since we have the place to ourselves, how about I show you and take you out for dinner afterwards?"

"I like the sound of that," Ellie said, as she filled a vase with water and arranged the roses in it.

"I'm going to talk to Kathryn. If she really wants that, she'll have to come to my house, and she'll have to leave when I ask her to. That seems to be the best way to handle this."

"What are you afraid of?" Ellie, smart and intuitive as always, asked.

"That I might see her point of view," Jordan answered, grateful to have Ellie's arms around her the next moment.

Chapter Six

After a phone call from Linwood Ashcroft early in the morning, Jordan agreed to a slight change of plans that benefited both her and Ellie. Linwood had offered to drive her if she could have someone pick her up later that day. Ellie was eager to do so since it would give them more time together while Derek and Kate were away.

Surprisingly, the younger Ashcroft brother showed lots of interest in her work.

"You know, I've been thinking a lot. Is it possible that your medical examiner made a mistake? I know my father. He didn't make any enemies, but he did have a lot of pride, wouldn't have told anyone if he was feeling weak or sick. He could get careless. Maybe that's what happened with those sleeping pills he took."

In the time since Jordan had studied up on Gerald Ashcroft, he struck her as many things—careless wasn't one of them. Besides, there was the matter of someone switching those pills for something far more dangerous. "At this time, the investigation doesn't support that theory," she said vaguely.

"If he got a new diagnosis, I wouldn't be surprised that he didn't tell anyone, not even Snyder. They're friends, but Dad was very...private."

Given the fact that they would spend at least another hour in the car together, Jordan decided to humor him.

"Do you have any reason to assume he might have seen another doctor? Did he mention it to you?"

Ashcroft kept his gaze on the road.

"He seemed...I don't know, worried, stressed. Of course, sadly, I didn't interpret the signs correctly. I think he was more fragile than he wanted all of us to believe."

That had not been the ME's interpretation, and Jordan was wondering why he wanted her to believe in it. Linwood had expected to take over the company. While he now owned a third, it wasn't going to be as easy as he might have thought. If he wanted his siblings out, he would have to buy them out.

"I guess you have a lot on your mind now, with the company and all," she ventured.

"Oh, tell me about it. I don't know what he was thinking, and to be honest, that makes me wonder about his mental health as well. All those charities...Whatever you think about it, we all know why he did that. Craig couldn't be trusted with money unless he had someone standing behind him, and Abby...Well, you know. She's not the most reliable person. This is going to be a constant tug of war with the two of them, and Craig will probably feel entitled since Dad was all up with those people who supported his dysfunctional lifestyle. What about you? Are you any closer to solving this? I mean...The more I think about it, the more I believe the department's resources aren't used the way they should be."

Ranting on, he hadn't noticed Jordan cringe at his use of the term "lifestyle."

"I still can't believe this was anything other than a sad accident. Dad probably meant for the stairs to get fixed a while ago, but Santos screwed that up. It was late at night, and he maybe got confused...Things happen at that age."

Jordan's sympathies were more with the dead man than with any of the people she found didn't seem to grieve all that hard.

They stopped for an early lunch on the way, and, half an hour later, arrived at Ashcroft's cabin, though the term was a bit of a euphemism, given the size of the two-story building.

It occurred to her that with all the luxury Ashcroft was surrounded with, he might have been pretty lonely. Then again, she knew firsthand that blood didn't always define family.

She spent most of the next hour going through every room, shadowed by her host. There were two glasses in the kitchen sink, one of them with a smear of lipstick. That was almost too easy. Fortunately, not every criminal was that clever, or taking precautions to cover up the crime they committed.

Ashcroft frowned at the find. "I'm not aware that he was seeing anyone. Santos got all googly-eyed in his presence, but other than that..."

Jealousy? Someone begrudged Ashcroft's wealth, him being well liked by everyone, his good health and possibly, a relationship. In any case, it was interesting that the housekeeper seemed to be more broken up about his death than anyone else.

There was an office with a huge desk, insurance papers scattered all over it. The memory on the phone showed that Ashcroft had placed calls from it to several companies.

"I don't understand," Linwood said. "He had people who would take care of that for him. Why would he do that?"

"There's only one way to find out," Jordan said as she jotted down the numbers. "We're going to ask them."

"You can do that? How do they know it's the police?"

"I won't get that kind of information from the call center staff that's there on the weekend. There's a procedure, but we will get our answers eventually."

"Oh, good. It's a fascinating job you have."

"It sure is."

She watched him open drawers and leaf through the papers inside.

"It looks like your father did a fair amount of work from this desk."

"No, most of these papers have to do with private matters."

A day planner caught Jordan's eye, and she picked it up, looking up the dates when Ashcroft had been in town for the last time. The pages were empty, save for one: Dr. T.

"Dr. T. You have any idea who that might be?"

"None whatsoever."

"Okay."

"That's all? You're not going to follow up on that?"

"Oh, we will, don't worry."

At this point, Jordan wondered who profited most from this little detour, and the scavenger hunt that was unfolding here.

Ellie enjoyed the drive into the rural, higher situated area, though she was still convinced it was a place for vacation rather than to live full-time. She found that a few hours worth of distance from the current problem had done wonders for Jordan, making her more relaxed.

It was still early in the day, and the drive along mountains and glittering lakes made her want to stay for a while longer.

"I'm sorry, I have to make a few calls and drop some things off at the lab. Another time," Jordan promised. "It's really beautiful."

"So how did it go?"

"Interesting. I'm pretty sure someone wanted me to go up there and find exactly what I found. It was too easy, pretty much all laid out for me."

"You think it was him?"

"Could be. Or someone else wanted to plant a little distraction."

"What if all those hints are legit, with or without someone pushing them on you?"

"I've thought about it. We'll know more next week. I believe that most of the people I need to talk to now won't be there on the weekend."

"Yeah, that's the only reason Kate could be convinced to go away...She's been working with a detective on that missing person case. No sign of life."

Between the two of them, she didn't need to say anything else. They all knew this wasn't good.

"How are you doing?" Ellie asked. "You're still okay with what you decided?"

"I guess. You all convinced me that it's for the best."

"Whatever happens, remember I'm here, okay?"

"I know," Jordan said.

The weekend was gone too soon, and instead of a breakfast at Kate and Ellie's, Jordan made do with a latte to go before she went to see Mrs. Santos. The housekeeper was still living at the mansion and probably would be for a while to come. Ashcroft had made sure that she could continue her duties even with new inhabitants.

She was wearing black again, her hair in a severe bun. It was obvious that she'd been crying.

"Mrs. Santos, I know you already answered a lot of questions. I won't take much more of your time."

"That's okay," she said, her voice heavy with tears. "I'm glad someone's willing to talk to me at least. The siblings usually look down their noses at me."

"Is that so? You've worked for their father a long time."

"Don't think they care. I heard them talk behind my back, whispering about whether I was working here legally. My mother was born in this country, and so was I. Of course, they never even bothered to ask, because when they came to see Gerald, it was always all about them, and the money they needed."

"Did he ever talk to you about these matters?"

"All the time. Dr. Snyder might pride himself in saying he was his best friend, but Mr. Ashcroft was different. He might have been in that old boy's club, because he came from old money, but those men weren't really his friends. Gerald was cut from a different cloth, kinder, of a more progressive mind than any of them. Nevertheless, he had to host them sometimes. He would share with me after those occasions that he was disgusted by most of it."

"I assume they would take issue with some of the charities he gave to?"

"You could say that. Look, my niece is a lesbian too. At first, I wasn't sure what to think about it, but Gerald and I had long talks, and he made me see that if you love someone, it doesn't matter at all."

"Did he ever take you to the cabin?"

Mrs. Santos hesitated.

"This is not a trick question. I'm just trying to see if there's anything you might have seen or overheard that could help us. You cared for Mr. Ashcroft a great deal, I know."

Unexpectedly, Mrs. Santos started to cry, and the next moment, Jordan found herself in an awkward embrace.

"It isn't fair," she sobbed. "We were supposed to have so much more time together."

"I'm sorry. You went with him the last time?"

"Yes. He was really worried about his offspring, as usual. Abby wanted money again, and someone in the company he had asked to take a look at things, found some irregularities in the books. It was all starting to add up."

"Could you give me the name of that person?"

"He said Chris. I assume he meant Coburn, who was working in the same department. He was over a few times."

"Thank you. Do you know if he saw a doctor while you two were there?"

Mrs. Santos stepped back, a surprised look on her face. "No, not one word. Of course, he could have...He left for town a couple of times, but I'm certain he would have told me."

"Okay, thank you so much. I'd like to take one more look around, and then I'll be gone."

"Suit yourself. I guess I need to call someone about those damn stairs."

Jordan spent another moment taking in the damage on the "damn stairs," before she drove to the department. A call to the lab confirmed that they had found the same set of prints on the glass with the lipstick stain and the day planner, Santos, Ashcroft, and another yet unidentified print on the planner.

Could there have been another woman? Maybe the kind older man had been a bit more of a player than they all assumed.

It seemed like everyone was telling their private little version of the truth, none of them giving her the big picture.

Darla Pierson had called her and asked to meet. Her former CI was now back in school and pregnant. Things were turbulent, but a lot more promising for her. Jordan was looking forward to seeing her.

She picked up the phone, intent on calling Kathryn and confronting her with an ultimatum right this moment but reconsidered. For this, she needed more of a plan.

"Hey, why don't you invite her over to our place?" Kate suggested, confusing Jordan for a moment until she realized Kate was talking about Darla. "We could all have dinner together."

Ellie and Kate had been guarding Darla at the hospital when she was in danger from an infamous crime lord. Darla might actually enjoy seeing them again, and Jordan would resign to the fact that those little gatherings were the new normal.

Her wish had been granted—she still had her own space. Those were small compromises, in comparison.

She wondered if Derek and Kate might have other plans at some point, but it was certainly too early to ask. For sure, she wouldn't let Ellie be homeless.

"Sure, I'll ask her."

"Cool. I like the *Night Shift*, but it's different from the *Code 7*. Lots of memories connected to that place." Kate didn't continue but looked very thoughtful all of a sudden.

"Takes some time," Jordan said. She didn't need more words to convey she understood that they all had lost a lot more than a favorite hangout.

Gerald Ashcroft's funeral attracted a sea of mourners, even more than Officer Jensen Baker's, the last one Jordan had to go to. The memory was creeping up on her. The rain. Bethany, nearly making a scene, and always close by but quiet and nearly invisible next to his father, Danny Roth, watching them, studying, choosing his victim.

Carl Roth had been a well-liked officer, and the *Code 7* was famous in the city, not just among cops. His son was an academy dropout who had blamed his failure on everyone but himself.

She focused her thoughts on the present. Whoever had wanted Gerald Ashcroft dead, it was very likely that this person was here among them.

Jordan noticed Abby and Craig sitting together with her daughter, Linwood in the same pew, but a bit further away next to the aisle. Mrs. Santos was in tears, as many of the attendants. Tamara Lyndon went over to Craig and Abby, and they spoke in hushed tones, their expressions serious. Linwood was watching them with interest.

He was the only one of the siblings to speak, and when he did, Jordan thought she detected a note of condescendence that irrationally angered her. It wasn't something she needed to care about, but it bothered her that Linwood showed this subtle disrespect for his father, for the legacy of creating hope for others who were less fortunate. Many representatives of charities had come to offer their condolences.

Linwood's wife sat stiffly next to her husband. Jordan had an idea of where she was coming from—Linwood's attitudes certainly didn't come from his family, so maybe his in-laws had made a difference. If that was the case, it hadn't deterred Gerald Ashcroft from giving to LGBT charities.

"Our father was a very giving man," Linwood said. "Sometimes, even giving too much."

That was probably not how he meant it to come across, but to Jordan, it sounded like complaining on a mighty high level. A third of the company and all assets within the house, plus the 300K would probably still leave him with more than his law firm made.

In the end, though, he was the only one who didn't have a financial motive.

Regardless of what Linwood had said, Jordan had asked Ellie to do some inquiries on her own and find out who could be the mysterious Dr. T. in Ashcroft's agenda. If someone had gone to all the trouble to present her with an elaborate puzzle, it would be interesting to see how the pieces fit together.

After the funeral, she and Derek went to see Chris Coburn, who, according to Mrs. Santos, had shadowed Craig because of suspicions his father had.

Coburn looked around nervously before he closed his office door behind them.

"I hope we can make this quick," he said. "In fact, I would prefer if no one even knew I talked to you. Now that Gerald's gone, I worry about my job here."

"Why is that?" Derek asked.

"What do you think? I'm sure Craig is already suspecting that I was the one who told Gerald about the recent irregularities. I tried to ask him if he had anything to do with all that shit—sorry about that."

Jordan, whom the apology was directed at, gave him a mild smile.

"Don't worry. Please continue."

"Anyway, there were some unaccounted sums, and I told Gerald about it. He was pretty heartbroken, but told me to let it go, and that he'd talk to Craig. I'm pretty sure he could tell where that was coming from."

"How recent?"

"A couple of weeks ago?"

Gerald Ashcroft had left shortly after for his trip to the cabin. To think about his next steps?

It looked like there was more they had to ask Craig about. Had the confrontation taken place after his father returned, and it got out of control? No. The setup with the stair showed premeditation.

They were back on the way to the department, where both the lab and Ellie hopefully had some results. Derek interpreted her sigh correctly.

"Don't you wish it was the homophobic one?"

"Yeah. But you can't arrest anyone for being an ass."

"True. Too bad sometimes."

Jordan thought about the lab results confirming Mrs. Santos' prints on both the glass and the agenda, and those of someone else besides Ashcroft's. Had Mrs. Santos not been aware, or was she lying? Jordan passed by Ellie who had been diligently making calls and crossing names off a list.

"Nothing so far," she said apologetically. "I widened the radius a bit, but there aren't that many Dr. T's to begin with, and the ones I spoke to, have never met Mr. Ashcroft."

"Thanks. Keep trying?"

"I will. Dinner with Darla tonight?"

"As long as nothing comes up, yes."

"Have you called Kathryn yet?"

"There was no time." At least, that wasn't an excuse. "I'll do it on the weekend." Maybe.

Odd that it was harder to confront her birthmother than her criminal biological father, but that's the way it was.

"We have to keep going," she said. "I'll see you later tonight."

⁂

"I can't help thinking you're showing a bit of a homophobic streak. Or are you so desperate for leads that you're grasping at straws?"

Jordan ignored Craig's accusation. "You only gave us bits and pieces of the truth, that's hardly a straw. You said those problems were in the past, and you and your father worked them out, but we've been told about recent occurrences. Is there anything you want to tell us about those, about the conversation you had with your father?"

"There was no conversation," Craig said angrily. "I hate to agree with Linwood on this one, but you're harassing my family. Please stop, or you'll hear from my lawyer."

"That's interesting. Linwood was very forthcoming. He invited me to come to the cabin."

"That's because you're an adult female, Detective. For Linwood, that's all it takes."

Jordan caught Derek's jaw drop, and she gave him a shrug. No, Linwood hadn't shown the slightest interest.

"You look surprised, Detectives. You really didn't know that he's been cheating on his wife from day one?"

"Your brother's moral conduct is not part of this investigation."

"But mine is? Yes, I had problems in the past. I took money out of the firm to help out Abby after Dad refused to invest in her business. I can legally do that, there's nothing wrong with it. I can show you the paperwork. I'd be very interested in who wanted to tie this to my old problems. I went to therapy for years. I did tell you the truth, I don't gamble anymore. Is that all?"

"One more thing." Jordan said. "We know that Mr. Ashcroft went to the cabin with Mrs. Santos the week before he died. There was another person with them. Do you have any idea who that might be?"

"That's your job, not mine, but I suggest you start looking somewhere other than this family. It's embarrassing. I have nothing more to say to you."

"Thank you, Mr. Ashcroft. That is all."

Chapter Seven

F rom where she was sitting, Ellie had a good vantage point
to observe the man striding purposefully to the lieutenant's office.

"Sir, can I help you?" she tried, but he ignored her, rapping at
the door. He was called in a moment later. Through the blinds
halfway open, she could see the tense body language of the two
men. This wasn't good. It was one of the Ashcroft sons, and
from the looks of it, he was not happy. She had the impression
that the detectives were making progress in the Ashcroft case,
and she herself had just gotten off the phone with a Dr. T, a
psychiatrist named Dr. Torres, who might be able to help them.

Nevertheless, there was a lot of pressure to solve this case
quickly, from the mayor's office, from the press. Sergeant Bristol
had brought in Jordan and Derek earlier to talk about the case.

Ellie wanted justice for every murder victim. She wanted to
be in Homicide for that reason. What she found hard to deal
with was that people put different priorities on investigations.
They were all equally important to her, the wealthy charitable
businessman just as much as a young woman who disappeared
off the street.

She had been distracted from her goals in the past months,
but she'd also set the vacation as a deadline to get back on track.
It wasn't that much longer until she'd be eligible to take the test.

She had been assigned to work with the detectives on numerous occasions. Things were starting to look up, for both her and Jordan.

Even better they not only could share their troubles, but their victories.

At the moment, neither Jordan nor Derek Henderson was anywhere to be seen. Ellie made a call to Jordan's cell and left her a message to call her back.

Ashcroft junior left the lieutenant's office, and shortly after, a woman entered the department, giving Ellie a smile as she looked around, and their eyes met. Blushing for no reason, Ellie looked away.

Kate who had witnessed the exchange, grinned, but Ellie's phone rang before she could say anything.

"What do you need?"

Ellie cleared her throat as the tone of Jordan's voice brought even more heat to her cheeks. That was, of course, completely irrational. Or maybe not.

"I...um...about your Dr. T. I think I found her. Dr. Torres, a psychiatrist outside of town. I kind of convinced the receptionist to confirm that they had a record of him—of course she wouldn't tell me anything, but I guess you won't have any problems getting the warrant. He might have shared any concerns or fears with her, so that could be important."

"I agree. Great job. Text me the address?"

"On its way. The doctor will be in until six today."

"You're the best. I'll be back in time for Darla. We order in?"

"I guess so. I'll see you then."

"Don't worry," Kate said. "She would have turned my head too."

"She didn't...Who is she anyway?"

"The new A.D.A., didn't you hear?"

Ellie vaguely remembered overhearing talk about the new arrival, Valerie Esposito. With her suit and high heels, the dark hair falling on her shoulders in waves, she looked like a character out of *Law & Order*.

"I didn't know it was today. Okay. What are you doing here?"

"I came to talk to a detective in missing persons...So far, I haven't been lucky. I see you made yourself comfortable here. You're still planning on taking the exam soon?"

"As soon as possible, yes."

"That's awesome. All right. I need to go. See you later."

"Yeah."

When Josh Ward had first attacked her on her way home from the *Code 7*, Ellie had decided to take life head on, no regrets. That attitude had served her well—it had started her relationship with Jordan. Now it was time to think of her career as well.

⌒◈₰

"Carpenter, Henderson, my office."

Given the fact that they had barely set foot into the room, this command didn't bode for good.

"I don't like the sound of that," Derek muttered, and Jordan wholeheartedly agreed. She had a bad feeling since they left Craig's office. Pre-emptively, she said, "Lieutenant, I was just going to call D.A. Hudson. We need a warrant for Mr. Ashcroft's patient file at a psychiatrist's..."

"You will do that, but could you explain to me why on her first day, A.D.A. Esposito has to deal with a possible lawsuit from Mr. Craig Ashcroft?"

"Yes, that wasn't what I expected, so I came here to hear what you had to say about it, detectives," Esposito said with a pleasant smile. "Of course, I can also look into that warrant for you, but you better have a good reason."

Jordan hadn't said anything since the lieutenant had interrupted her, and Derek was silent as well. The silence dragged on, turning awkward.

"Nice to see you two again," Valerie Esposito finally said. "Now, about that complaint..."

"We have a witness who confirmed Craig took money out of the business recently. Both he and Mr. Ashcroft senior had suspicions as to where this money went. According to Craig Ashcroft, he used it to help his sister. We had to check on that," Jordan defended their strategy.

"Of course you had, but I can't stress enough how important it is to be cautious with this family. I understand there hasn't been an arrest yet?" Valerie's tone made it sound like a rhetorical question. "Are you even close?"

"You both said to tread carefully," Derek said. "That's what we're doing. Some family members obviously had money problems."

"I take that as a no." She sighed. "Okay then. Whoever was in that cabin with Mr. Ashcroft and Mrs. Santos, find them. Mr. Ashcroft junior thought there might have been a homophobic undertone to the conversation. Please don't do that. If he's the one, we don't want him to look sympathetic in any way."

"That's all," the lieutenant added. "Now get back to work."

"I'm done here too." The A.D.A. got to her feet. "Detective Carpenter can walk me out?"

"No problem."

Jordan got to her feet and followed her outside, not sure if she should be relieved.

"Relax," Valerie Esposito said when they had reached the double doors. "I got an opportunity to come back, and I took it. It had nothing to do with you."

"That's...great."

"I hear you moved out, pulled yourself together. Good for you. I look forward to working with you."

"Yeah, me too," Jordan said after the slightest bit of hesitation, which hadn't gone unnoticed with Valerie. "You heard these things where?"

"Here and there. It doesn't matter. I guess I see you around?"

It would be hard to avoid.

"Dr. Torres will be in her office until six. You think you'll have the warrant for me before that?"

"I'll get right on it. Don't make me come back here for the Ashcrofts, unless you have a solid arrest, okay?"

"I promise."

"It's good to see you again, Jordan." Valerie Esposito left, and for a moment, Jordan couldn't help but wonder about the irony of fate, or coincidence.

"I'm not sure if I can help you much. Mr. Ashcroft came to see me because he had a mild case of anxiety. He had trouble sleeping, and nothing he'd tried had worked. I prescribed a mild sleeping aid. As you know he was involved with various charities, but he worried about not doing enough, and what might happen with his children if he wasn't around."

Fortunately, Dr. Torres was more forthcoming. "We only had a couple of sessions."

"Did he ever mention concerns about being threatened?"

"No, his family was all he talked about. You wouldn't be able to use that in court, but he was worried about the relationship between the brothers. The younger one married into a very conservative family, and there were regular arguments because his older brother is gay. He also stopped giving money to his daughter after the umpteenth business idea flopped. He didn't worry about their financial future, but more about his legacy. He cared deeply about these causes."

"More than about his family?" Derek asked.

Dr. Torres shrugged. "The people he worked with were always grateful. They never disappointed him. What do you think?"

She was right, Jordan reflected. This added to the picture they had already established so far, but it didn't give them anything new.

"In any case, he thought Craig and Abigail might go as far as embezzle from the firm, and that Craig was in on the scheme to finance a relapse in his gambling. He talked about all this during his last visit, and he was pretty upset about it, but as far as I can tell, he had no real evidence. He wondered if he might be too paranoid about these things, and we talked about what he could do to find some distance. Not about the business, that's not my forte."

Ashcroft had at least been partly right, and Coburn's findings confirmed that.

It was still unclear who could have been the third person in the cabin. Torres had no idea.

⁂

When they arrived at Kate and Ellie's apartment, Darla Pierson was already there, greeting Jordan with a hug.

"Hey. You're still busy, I see."

"And you're almost due."

"Tell me about it." Darla sighed. "I can't believe it's going to be another nine weeks."

"You look great though." Jordan said, catching Ellie watching them with a smile. It was true, she had reacted quickly and unfairly at first, and she was lucky Darla had forgiven her.

The first twelve years of her life had had an impact, making it hard for Jordan to believe that an unexpected pregnancy could ever be a blessing, and that someone this young could be ready to be a parent. Surprisingly, Darla had grabbed her new life with all its opportunities and challenges with both hands.

Being confronted with her own childhood had been uncomfortable, reminding her that at one time, she could have taken a similar path. Jordan was lucky to have been dealt better cards along the way.

"Thank you."

Ellie got up to get a juice for Darla and a beer for everyone else, while Kate passed the takeout menu around. After everyone made their choice, she called the Italian restaurant.

It was a relief to see that Darla would be okay. It was odd to think that some of Ashcroft's money might have gone into one of the programs that helped her shape her own future.

The Ashcroft siblings all had started out with so much privilege, the means to lead comfortable lives while making those of others better. Yet, one had become a homophobe, one was aggressively making false accusations, and one seemed unable to make her ideas reality.

How much had they resented their father for giving in other places?

What conversations went on now behind closed doors?

⁓

The space next to her in the bed was empty, though still warm. Ellie got out of bed and put on a robe. She didn't have to go far: Jordan stood by the window in the kitchen. She had turned on the light of the hood above the stove, on low, as to not disturb the other occupants of the apartment.

"Can't sleep?" Ellie asked softly.

"Just thinking. I'm sorry if I woke you. You need a good night's sleep too."

Ellie knew she'd have a better chance with Jordan by her side, but it was no secret that both of them had a lot on their minds.

"It's okay. I'm fine." She stepped closer, into Jordan's arms, and they stood like that for a moment before they both took a seat at the table.

"It's one of the weirdest cases I ever worked on," Jordan said, sounding frustrated. "One of them thinks being gay is a dysfunctional lifestyle, the 'you're going to hell' kind—the other one actually accused me of being homophobic."

"Wow." Ellie didn't have much more to say to that.

"And the sister, she's somewhere in between, but all of them are...off. That doesn't mean they killed anybody, but they are sure starting to give me a headache. Their father just died—according to everyone else who knew him, a saint. There they are complaining about how he was spending too much money on charities."

"Privilege can be blinding," Ellie offered. "Not that it's an excuse. In fact, it's damn cold. And they seem eager to blame everyone but themselves, for just about everything. Do you think they did commit any crimes, other than murder? It seems to me that they're all cocky enough to think they could get away with a lot."

"I'm not sure. Craig had this gambling problem, but he swears it's over. Abigail has lots of shiny ideas but doesn't see them through. And Linwood is not happy about having to share with them. I wouldn't be surprised if they start accusing one another soon."

"Could it be somebody from the outside?" Ellie asked. The puzzle intrigued her. "Whatever people say, he must have pissed off more people than just his offspring. Those charities...He was making a pretty big political statement with his choices."

"Yeah, not what you would expect from a rich old white guy...but apparently, he was the real deal, a good Samaritan. Too bad his own family couldn't see that."

"That bothers you?"

Jordan laughed, surprised at the question. "It doesn't bother you?"

"I don't know. It's not personal. I know my family, my values...I'm sorry. I feel like I'm overstepping."

"No, you're right." Jordan sighed. "It's stunning to me. I don't even feel that way about Kathryn. At least I hope I don't."

"I know you don't. You're a better person than that."

"It's debatable if either of you is a good person." Kate came into the kitchen, yawning. "There's no coffee. I thought we had a rule—who gets up first, makes it."

"It's that late already? Oh, crap." With dismay, Ellie realized there would be no time to continue their conversation in bed. A moment later, the shower came on.

"You've got to be kidding me," Jordan muttered. "All right. I'm going to make it. It doesn't look like anyone is getting a shower around here anytime soon."

Kate laughed. "You are all so cranky in the morning. I see a whole new side of you all with these living arrangements."

Ellie caught Jordan's gaze on her, realizing that she, like all of them, was grateful for this bit of lightness and banter. They had made good choices. They would build on them—and figure out who had hated Gerald Ashcroft enough to end his life and legacy.

Chapter Eight

E llie and Casey had barely pulled out of the department's parking lot when the 911 call came in: A jogger had found an unconscious woman in an alleyway. They arrived seconds after the ambulance, two paramedics heading for the figure lying beneath the fire escape. The jogger, in her thirties, stood on the other side of the alley, clutching her cell phone.

"Thank God you're here. I'm Teresa, I called 911." Her words came out in breathless gasps. "She's not dead, is she?"

Ellie recognized the paramedic kneeling next to the pale, unmoving woman, Marietta Bruno. She looked at Ellie and shook her head. Casey was taking Teresa aside while Marietta's colleague tended to her.

Ellie took in the dead woman, noticing the bruises around her neck and arms. She'd have to make a call.

Afterwards, she went over to Casey and the witness. Teresa, while shocked about the turn of events, related how she had found the woman. "I can't believe I was late this morning. I always take this route, same time, every day. If I'd found her earlier..."

"It's likely that it wouldn't have made a difference," Ellie said softly. The woman must have been out there for a few hours, she guessed. Other people, residents, must have come by?

"You can't be sure."

No. One small decision, a left turn, could make a big difference at times.

"We'll be sure soon. What do we have, Harding?"

Ellie followed Detective Maria Doss who had just arrived. "Caucasian female, thirties, has bruises on her arms and around her neck. I didn't see any ID. She's not wearing a coat or a purse, so...maybe a mugging gone bad."

"We'll get to that, thank you," Doss said. Ellie wondered if there had been a subtle reproach in her voice. Before Henderson started going out with Kate, he had briefly dated Maria Doss, which connected them all in an odd awkward way—but this wasn't about any of them.

"I didn't mean to suggest..."

"That's okay. It could be." Donning latex gloves, she crouched next to the body, carefully turning the woman's wrist to show the marks went all around. The medical examiner's van pulled up as well.

"Or not," Doss continued. "Look. She was tied up. Are you going to throw up?" she asked, matter-of-factly, without any judgment.

Ellie caught herself. "No. I promise. That just caught me off guard."

"Good. Get some backup here. I need you guys to canvass the neighborhood, see if anyone saw anything."

She pointed to tire tracks a few feet away. "See how wide those are?"

"They don't look like they belong to any of the cars around here, I would assume. He dumped her." Ellie said.

"Nice. Now see if anyone has heard or, hopefully seen, a big truck passing through last night."

"I'm on it. Detective Waters isn't here?"

Maria Doss looked surprised, but she gave an answer anyway. "No, doing some work on Carpenter and Henderson's case. Isn't everybody these days?"

It was a fair question, Ellie thought.

Changes. Some of them were for the better. Some of them were unavoidable, and you had to roll with the punches. After her shift that night, Jordan decided to get it over with and make that call. She would treat this like a doctor's appointment—unpleasant but necessary for your health in the long run.

Still, Jordan sat in her car for about five minutes before she clicked the number.

Kathryn picked up on the second ring.

"Hey," Jordan said, wishing she had developed more of a plan beforehand.

"It's you! I'm so happy you decided to call. How are you? Does this mean we can meet?"

The jarring contrast of past and present was enough to get her back on track.

"I'm fine. I still can't tell what you're trying to achieve with this, but several people I trust have convinced me to give it a shot. Since it's the only way I can get you to stop texting me."

Kathryn was silent on the other end. This maybe meant that for the first time, she was actually listening. She had better.

"I will meet you, but not right away. You have to give me until the end of the month, and you will come to my house, on a Friday or Saturday evening. I'll listen to what you have to say, and that's it."

"I was hoping we could..." Kathryn sighed. "There's a lot you don't know. Jim tells me to let it go, that we can't undo the past, but..."

"He has a point there."

"Would it be so bad if I was in your life now? I've seen what you've become, and sweetie, I'm so proud—"

"No." Jordan took a deep breath. "That's not how it works. You'll come to my house, say what you have to say. I'll give you an hour or even two. Make your case if you must. I have a family."

"Is it that you're ashamed of your real family?"

"What real family are you talking about? TJ? Jim? No, I'm not ashamed. Do you want to know why? It's because I have nothing in common with any of you. I'm actually grateful. The fact that you never cared, never tried to find me—it was good for me. It was such a relief when I realized I'd never have to go back."

"I don't want that. I want to know you in the present. You're still my daughter."

"That's convenient, isn't it? I have to go. Let's say Friday in two weeks, five o'clock. If you're not there, I'll assume you changed your mind."

"I won't. Thank you, Jordan. You'll never know how much this means to me."

I'm afraid you're right.

Intentionally or not, Kathryn knew how to choose words that hit too close to home, Jordan thought as she walked into the *Night Shift*. It was true that she firmly believed she was lucky to be very different from her blood relatives, or even Jim, the present but unengaged father she had known in her first twelve years. TJ Pratt—yes, she had harbored all kinds of negative feelings since finding out that he was her biological parent, and shame might have been one of them. After the Darby case, her focus had been on proving to her colleagues and supervisors that she still could do her job. The discovery had jeopardized that focus, and she wasn't proud of any of it.

She didn't feel like hanging out at the *Night Shift* tonight, so instead she took Ellie aside and asked, "Could we go somewhere else?"

"Hello to you too. Tough day?"

They hadn't seen each other since the morning. Jordan knew Ellie had been busy with one of Doss's crime scenes. "I'm sure yours was tougher, but I'd like to be somewhere alone with you. Would that be okay?"

"Of course." Ellie smiled, but the worried tone belied her initial reaction. "Did you call Kathryn?"

That was almost scary. "Yes." Jordan sighed. "I guess it went okay. I made a date with her in two weeks."

"Two weeks." Ellie frowned.

"Well, yeah, I'm kind of busy right now."

"I understand that, but…Okay. I guess you need some prep time for that conversation. Do you want me to be there?"

Jordan was tempted by the offer. She shook her head.

"I don't think that would be a good idea. Like you said, I'll brace myself, and it'll be okay. I have a pretty good idea of what she's going to say. I can't do this with the Ashcroft case still open."

Ellie nodded, but Jordan understood what she wasn't saying. There was no guarantee the case would be closed a couple of weeks from now.

"I promise, I won't change my mind. The sooner I do this, the sooner we can all move on. Let's go?"

"Sure. Where to?"

"Oh, hi. I see this is the place to be these days. Can you recommend anything on the menu?" Valerie Esposito asked cheerfully.

"I'm sorry, we were just leaving," Jordan said, taking Ellie's hand in an unmistakable gesture. "Ellie?"

"I'm coming." To Esposito, Ellie said, "I'm Ellie Harding, by the way. Welcome. We haven't come here often, yet, but the veggie pizza is pretty good."

"Great, I'll give it a try. See you."

Jordan was now even more in a hurry to leave. When they were out on the sidewalk, she asked, "What just happened?"

"Why?" Ellie's question sounded completely innocent, and it probably was. "I saw her earlier at the department. Kate told me she's the new A.D.A. Something I should know about her?"

"Not really." *Another time. Maybe.* "Okay, where do we go?"

"I don't mind, as long as they serve food. I'm starving." They walked a bit further down the block until they reached a bistro/bar that had a small discreet rainbow flag in the window. Named after its owners Dan and Teddy, the *D&T* was new in town and promised a happy hour until midnight.

"Let's try this?"

Ellie studied the dishes written on the chalkboard sign critically and gave her okay.

The waitress led them to a table in the back and after a quick check of the menu, Ellie ordered a beer, Jordan a Long Island Iced Tea.

"Whoa. Are you going to tell me about that phone call?"

"It wasn't all that bad," Jordan assured her. "All I wanted was to be alone with you and have a drink in peace." She sighed. "Okay, you're right. I know what it's going to be like. She's going to want me to see sense in something that doesn't make sense. She and Jim screwed up, big time. There were other options. They just bided their time and did whatever they wanted until Child Protective Services knocked on their door. There is no other side to that story. That is the story."

"The story isn't going to change."

"I hope you're right."

Ellie took a sip from Jordan's cocktail. "Hm, that is good. We're going to take a cab later?"

"You're going to come with me?"

Ellie's gaze softened. "Of course."

No, the story wouldn't change. It would always end with the two of them together. They had been through worse than an unwanted family reunion. *This too shall pass.*

When they left, there was a younger couple coming in at the same time, obviously just starting their night. Ellie had the same thought.

"Doesn't it make you cringe? I used to be like that in college. Now it's a drink or two, and I can't wait to curl up in bed." She reconsidered and added, "On the other hand...I can curl up in bed with you. That's better than anything."

"You weren't drinking in college while you were underage, right?" Jordan teased.

"Right. Let's go home now."

"Yeah."

Jordan cast one last look at the couple who seemed to be fighting now, in low hushed tones. That made her cringe even more. She knew what it was like to be caught up in a bitter exchange like that—she'd been there with Bethany often enough, her attempts at escaping always bringing her back to the same place.

Not anymore. This time, she was the lucky one.

She watched as Ellie put on her coat. A third woman had arrived out of nowhere, and now the argument was getting louder, voices raised. She pushed one of the others, getting pushed in return, and one of the barstools crashed to the floor, the two of them exchanging slurs.

"Really?" Ellie said, exasperated.

"Yes, really. Come on." They had reached the fighting women within a few steps.

"Hey, take it easy," Jordan said, earning glares from both of them.

"What's it to you?" said one.

"She's been trying to hook up with my girlfriend," the other one accused.

The girlfriend sat on one of the stools at the counter, regarding the scenery with unease.

"Well maybe you should ask yourself why."

They were a hair's breadth away from throwing punches, but Jordan flashing her badge put the argument to a halt quickly.

"What the hell? Police? We were just talking."

"Yeah, try to do it without damaging the furniture or yourselves, okay?" Ellie said.

"We don't have to call it in if you stop it right here," Jordan added. "We're cool?"

The one accused of trying to steal the other one's girlfriend gave her a long look. "I assume we are. I was going to leave anyway. Your loss," she scoffed towards the woman on the barstool, nearly starting the fight again.

"Relax," Jordan warned. "Let her go. You guys sort out what you need to sort out. Have a good night."

"They don't seem very grateful," Ellie observed when they made their way to the exit once more, casting a look over her shoulder. "All of a sudden I'm not so jealous anymore."

"Good." Jordan laughed. "How about we go home and proceed as planned? Curling up in bed sounds really good right now. I hope no one starts taking the bar apart when we're gone."

"Yeah, having to look for another new place, that would suck. How about we go to my apartment?" Ellie suggested. "It's easier to get to work tomorrow. We could carpool."

"Oh yeah, sure."

"Don't laugh."

"I'm not laughing. I never knew Henderson was so damn cheerful in the morning."

"I'll make it up to you," Ellie said. "You know that."

Jordan loved the insinuation in her words. *All right then.*

"I can't wait," she said.

Even a little tipsy, they managed to keep their hands to themselves in the cab nonetheless. In the elevator, however, all bets were off. From there until they finally closed the door of Ellie's room, it was all a blur. Between them, they still had a fair amount of need for reassurance, in their relationship, in the aftermath of recent events.

Making love always worked for them.

In the morning, Jordan was almost disappointed to realize she wouldn't be able to start the workday over breakfast. Kate joined them at the table, looking bleary-eyed, but Derek wasn't there.

Jordan couldn't help worrying she might have overlooked something at the scene, something that would make the M.O. clearer, that would bring them ahead in a way they desperately needed. As long as Mrs. Santos was in the house, she didn't think it would be a problem—she just had to make sure Craig didn't know about it.

"Derek stayed at his own place last night. Court today." Kate yawned.

Jordan suppressed a sigh. So he would be out for most of the day.

"You're going to need me for something today?" Ellie asked, making her think of various ways, none of which had to do with work.

Jordan cleared her throat. "Actually yes. I'd like to go over to the Ashcroft house one more time. I have a feeling."

"I hear the new A.D.A. wants everyone to be extra careful," Kate said. It wasn't much of a question where she'd heard that.

"I will be. I'd like you to look over the sibling's finances once more. There has to be something."

"Sorry." Kate shrugged. "I'll be over in Missing Persons this morning. We're still looking. No sign of her so far."

"I'll talk to Bristol. If the lieutenant wants this case solved so badly, he needs to have people on it."

"Can't Waters..."

"Detective Waters is busy otherwise, believe me."

"Okay," Ellie chimed in. "I guess breakfast is over. Let's go."

Chapter Nine

E llie was relieved that the tone had stayed amiable. She knew
Kate didn't like Jordan making decisions like this, after
she'd invested a lot in the case of the missing college student.
She also knew Jordan was stressed, about the slow progress
and many obstacles in the Ashcroft case, and about Kathryn.
Hopefully, their friendship could remain intact.

She was aware that living with Kate was some sort of limbo,
until she had figured out if she wanted to be with Derek in the
long run or not, until Jordan wasn't too skittish anymore to
let somebody else into her space, without the fear of another
suffocating entanglement.

Nevertheless, it wasn't a bad arrangement, biding time for all
of them.

Only, sometimes, Ellie thought she was the one who needed
that time least. She had made up her mind a long time ago.

She was distracted from her thoughts when they reached the
driveway of the Ashcroft mansion.

"Wow. The things that money can buy."

"Yeah. Happiness and a long life obviously aren't some of
them."

"Well, I don't have the money, but I certainly have the happiness. And I plan to be around for some time to come."

"That's good to know," Jordan said. "Okay, let's do this."

A car with a distinct logo was parked in front of the building. Mrs. Santos opened the door to them on the first ring.

"Detective! Do you have any news? Have you found out who murdered Gerald?"

"Not yet, unfortunately."

"Is the press bothering you again? You can send them away, you know?" they heard a voice from the kitchen. "Or I can do it for you. Oops. I guess you guys have a reason to be here. Officers."

Ellie noticed that Jordan didn't make an attempt to clarify rank. She noticed something else, too—the young woman was one half of the couple from the *D&T*.

"Detective Carpenter, this is my niece Aleja," Mrs. Santos said. "She was helping me sort out my papers...I'm not sure if I can stay in this house. Sure, Gerald said I could, but his children are going to fight this, so...I could use the money to find me somewhere else to live. That poor man. I don't think they're going to use this place at all like he intended."

"His will is binding," Jordan reminded her.

"There are always loopholes. How can I help you?"

"I'd like to take a look at Mr. Ashcroft's suite again," Jordan said. "By the way, could you tell me who the car outside belongs to?"

So she had noticed the logo too.

"It's mine," Aleja said. Leaning against the doorway, she had watched the exchange with interest. "Well, not actually mine. I was about to go to work from here. I'm a pharma sales rep."

"That's interesting. You're promoting new medications and treatments to clinics and practices? I imagine that's tough."

"Not harder than solving a murder, I think." Aleja gave Ellie a cordial smile. "My firm sells a variety of medication for severe chronic conditions, the kind where there's always lots of costs involved. Everyone's looking for solutions."

"You sell Digoxin too?"

"Among many others, yes."

"You have samples with you right now?"

Aleja laughed. "What, Detective, are you thinking of changing careers?"

"It would really help if I could see the sample right now," Jordan said, her tone level and polite.

Ellie could tell that the younger woman was about to argue but thought otherwise. Probably she was worried they could tell her aunt about the fight she'd gotten into.

"Is anything wrong?" Mrs. Santos asked.

"Don't worry," Aleja said. "I'm sure the ladies here simply need my expertise. Right?"

"That's absolutely right. Thank you."

Back outside, Ellie watched as Aleja produced a sample of the drug.

"I assume this is not something to come by easily," Jordan said, still making conversation.

"Oh, no. Like everything that can be quite dangerous in the wrong hands. Kind of like guns. No offense."

"Would you mind if I keep this?"

"Normally I would say yes, but since it doesn't seem like you're going to rat me out to my aunt about the bar fight, sure, keep this. I assume you're not going to tell me what for."

"Did you know Mr. Ashcroft?" Jordan asked.

"Yes, sure, I saw him around when I came to visit my aunt. For a rich old white guy, he was pretty cool, I guess. You probably heard that he supported various organizations, including LGBT charities. He was always friendly to me."

"And with your aunt?"

Aleja gave her a wry smile. "I assume you figured that out too, didn't you?"

Ellie wondered where Jordan was going with this, and if she really believed Aleja could be involved in Ashcroft's death. She waited, and eventually, Aleja continued.

"They're adults, right, they can do whatever they want. I have no problem with that. His kids, however, they were often quite nasty with her. I guess now that he gave her money, that's not going to end anytime soon."

"Okay. Thank you, Aleja."

Back in the car, Ellie said, "All right, I get part of your theory. If Ashcroft had been as bad to her as the siblings, or if he was involved with another woman, one of them could have gotten to these pills. He seemed to have been a good guy, to everyone. For Mrs. Santos, and, or Aleja, there's still no motive."

"I know," Jordan said. "But there are plenty of people with a motive to frame them."

Searching Ashcroft's suite didn't turn up anything new, and besides, Jordan was eager to share their findings.

"That's...a theory," the lieutenant said when she stood in his office half an hour later. "Can we prove it? Anything?"

Jordan suppressed a sigh. She had already known that his reaction wouldn't be quite as enthusiastic as Ellie's, and the "we" was as much slack as he would cut her.

"All siblings had a complicated relationship with their father."

"I have a complicated relationship with my kids. Try again, Carpenter."

"We went over everything, his business relations, the charities, everyone who knew him loved him. He was one of the rare examples of someone highly privileged who put his money to good. The only people who didn't profit from that, as much as they wanted to anyway, were his children. The psychiatrist confirmed that this was his main concern, that they took the wealth for granted. Now, Mrs. Santos' niece is the first person in the circle who had access to the drug that debilitated Mr. Ashcroft. She has no motive, but she drives a company car, and she had samples in the car."

"Did she mention that anything was missing, or stolen recently?"

"No."

That was a detail that didn't sit well with Jordan either. If Aleja had noticed drugs missing, but not reported them, it could mean she was trying to protect her aunt.

"Then make sure that is not the case. You said it yourself, this is the first connection to the drug. That's not a coincidence."

"I agree, sir, but..."

"I want you to concentrate on that angle. Thanks, Detective. That would be all."

Jordan returned to her desk, unsure whether she should be frustrated or encouraged about this new development. Clearly, many people they had talked to had left out inconvenient parts of the truth. Did Mrs. Santos have no idea about the specifics of her niece's job, or had she deliberately not mentioned them? And Aleja...Judging from the scene at the *D&T*, she could be aggressive, but, in Jordan's opinion, that wasn't enough to make her a good suspect. The murder of Ashcroft showed planning, very unlike punching someone in public.

Still, she couldn't ignore that Aleja was the one who was aware of the effects the drug would have.

Either way, it wasn't a coincidence. She called Kate to see if she had found anything in the siblings' financial records.

Monday morning came with unexpected tensions as Jordan's theory became less likely. Doss had been able to ID the victim in her murder case, and she had last been seen leaving the *D&T* with another woman. The bartender had made a positive ID: Aleja Santos. She was brought in and waiting for Doss in an interrogation room.

Now Aleja was connected to two homicides happening within less than a month, which didn't bode well for her.

"I'm coming with you," Jordan declared.

Maria shrugged. "Help yourself. As my partner and every other cop is still busy on *your* case..."

"We don't make the assignments, Maria."

"I didn't mean to suggest otherwise. Come on."

"All right."

Aleja breathed a sigh of relief when she saw Jordan walking into the room.

"Thank God you're here. You're going to tell them it's all a misunderstanding, right? I didn't kill anybody."

"Detective Doss here needs to ask you a few questions, okay?"

"If it's just a few questions, why am I here?" Aleja asked suspiciously. "Shouldn't I call a lawyer?"

Jordan doubted that she had her own lawyer. "If you feel at any time that you did something that requires legal assistance, sure, a public defender will be here for you. For now, it's just that—questions."

Maria's expression had gone from surprised to impatient.

"Can we do this now? We have witnesses that saw you leave a bar, the *D&T*, with Sandra Paulson. Apparently, you were the last one to see her alive."

"Before the person who killed her, you mean." Aleja's eyes filled with tears. "I have no idea what happened to her. We parted ways, she said she'd call me when she got home, but she never did. I assumed she had forgotten. We didn't really know each other all that well. That's what it's like with the people you meet at the *D&T*. You can ask your colleague here."

"Something you want to add to that, Jordan?" Maria asked mildly.

"If you want to talk about that night, Aleja? I was there with my girlfriend, not that it's any of your concern's, or Detective Doss's, for that matter. You nearly got thrown out for starting a fight."

"I'd like to hear more of that."

Aleja shook her head. "You're just as bad as the Ashcrofts, not the old man, I mean, but his offspring. They always expect the worst of me and my aunt."

"Right now, you're the only person connecting two murder cases. This is a fact, not anybody's expectation. It would help if you told the whole truth."

"There is nothing else! Sandra came on to me in that bar. We had fun together. I never expected us to start dating, but I thought it was shitty that she never even called...Of course I didn't know someone murdered her. Damn it. I went back to the bar. I hung out with another girl, and then her girlfriend showed up. You know the rest," she said to Jordan to whom this testimony sounded oddly familiar. She had seen her fair share of relationship drama. Being with Ellie was smooth sailing in comparison, even with the obstacles thrown in their way from the start.

"We helped contain the situation," she explained to Maria. "At that time, we didn't know about Aleja's job or the fact that she was connected to Paulson. Aleja, is there anything you can remember about the night you went out with her? Somebody she talked to, anything?"

"Not really. I just thought it was strange...she was very focused from the first moment. Like she came in and had it all figured out that moment. I realized it probably wasn't the first time for her, picking up someone like that, but I didn't mind. I believe in serial monogamy. As long as the person is not otherwise involved, it's cool."

Jordan uncomfortably felt like this young kid was giving her a lesson in relationship etiquette, and someone she knew would have a field day with that. Fortunately, she didn't get to analyze Jordan's mistakes any longer.

"Let me talk to Detective Doss for a second. Don't worry, Aleja. We're grateful for your help."

"Don't worry, Aleja?" Maria echoed once they were outside the door. "Okay, first of all, I didn't say you could question her. Given the fact that I was going to ask those questions, oh well, I can let that go."

"I'm sorry. Henderson never lets me be the good cop." Jordan realized too late that this joke was seriously misplaced with Maria. "Okay. I'm really sorry. That was probably uncalled for. For the record, I didn't approve the way my partner—"

"It's fine. I wasn't going to discuss this with you, now, or ever. Let's go back to what just happened. What is your angle?"

"My angle is that she had no motive, with Ashcroft or Paulson. Her aunt, the housekeeper, was romantically involved with Mr. Ashcroft. He was apparently kind to her, and he invested in LGBT charities. Aleja liked him. As for Sandra Paulson, why would she want to kill a woman she had a one-night stand with? That doesn't make sense."

"You think? You said it yourself, she started a fight. The situation had to be contained. It doesn't look to me like she was planning to kill anyone, but the situation might have gotten out of hand. And she's connected to your high-profile case."

Jordan shook her head.

"So you think she was acting impulsively? That's not what happened with Ashcroft. No, someone wants her to look like a good suspect. I just don't know yet, why. Mrs. Santos wants to leave the house, so she doesn't have to deal with the siblings' antics any longer. She got some money, but not an outrageously high sum. I'm coming back to the lack of motive, for both of them."

"If I find you that motive, will you give up on your conspiracy theory?"

"Sure. I don't think you will, though."

"You're ready to let me finish this?"

"Yeah. I promise I will keep my mouth shut."

Aleja left the department minutes later. At least she wasn't threatening to sue. It had become an unsettlingly familiar part of the day.

To Jordan's surprise, Craig Ashcroft came in later that day, asking to talk to her. "What can I do for you?" she asked, hoping this conversation wouldn't end in another stern reproach from the lieutenant.

"Thanks for seeing me, Detective. I came here to apologize. Some of the things I said…I understand you're doing your job. So—I'm sorry."

"I appreciate that," Jordan said, fairly baffled. "It's a difficult time for your family."

"You could say that. Dealing with my father's death has not been easy. Dealing with my siblings…You can imagine. When you suggested that any of us could have something to do with this, I snapped. I didn't mean to." He hesitated long enough for the pause to become awkward, before he said, "I realize we're family too, in a way. It's not easy to be out at work, to everyone."

"Mr. Ashcroft, thank you." Jordan didn't want to confirm nor deny anything, though she was asking herself where he could have gotten that information. "Since you're here, can I ask you a question?"

"Of course."

"Mrs. Santos' niece, Aleja, do you know her? Does she come around often?"

"Oh, sure. She actually came out to me before she told her aunt. Why? Do you think she has something to do with my father's death?"

"Just curious. If you excuse me now, I have to…"

"Yes, sure, you're at work. We're good?"

"Yes," she said, giving him a polite smile. "We're good."

"Oh, before I forget about it. Abigail asked me to give you this." He handed her an envelope imprinted with gold and purple. "It's an invitation. She's launching her cosmetics line, and she thought you might be interested. You can bring a plus one." He laughed wistfully. "Yeah, the timing might be odd, but she wants to dedicate this to Dad. He helped her out so much, it would serve no one if she just gave it up. Can I tell her you'll come?"

"I'll think about it. Thanks."

She watched him leave, then turned to the notes on her desk, containing every aspect of the "conspiracy theory."

"What the hell was that about?"

Chapter Ten

T he bad news kept coming for Aleja. She had no alibi. Her DNA was all over Sandra Paulson's body. In a storage unit Aleja had rented, Doss and Waters had discovered rope crusted in blood, under a plastic tarp, and a set of tires which matched the tracks found in the alley where Sandra Paulson had been left.

"This is too much of a coincidence, don't you see that?"

Jordan still believed in her theory, and she had no trouble opposing the opinion held by the lieutenant, the other detectives, and A.D.A. Esposito.

"It's all there," Waters said. "The owner ID'd her. She doesn't deny everything else in there belongs to her. Books, tools, some furniture. You might want to take a look too. There's a lot of medical stuff there."

"If she was such a clever mastermind, don't you think she would have hidden some of it better?"

"She used an alias," Valerie said. "Maybe she got in over her head. Paulson might have found out that she killed Ashcroft and tried to blackmail her—"

"None of which we can prove."

"And she needed to get rid of the witness," the A.D.A. continued, unfazed by Jordan's interruption. "Jordan, I can understand that after all you've been through, you hate to see a young woman go down for this, but these are the facts. We have her on

Paulson. If she didn't act alone, we could help her somewhat if she gave up that other person."

"You're thinking about Mrs. Santos? That's ridiculous."

"Carpenter," the lieutenant scolded. "A.D.A. Esposito will go forward with the Paulson case. If there's another charge to add, you better bring it soon."

"There's something else," Valerie said. "I'm going to need you to testify what you saw that night in the bar."

Just like that, all eyes were on her. This day was quickly heading towards bizarre, Jordan thought. Like she'd told Ashcroft junior earlier, her workplace wasn't hostile. That didn't mean she wanted to detail her activities after work in a courtroom.

She regretted taking Ellie there, based on a few rave reviews about the cocktails.

"If that's what you need. I'm going to take a look at what you found in that storage unit. You think she locked her in there?"

Jordan still had a hard time believing Aleja had strangled the woman with her bare hands.

"It's likely. We're going to find out soon."

Instead of the *Night Shift*, she had agreed to another night at Kate and Ellie's. It was practical, but it also meant a lot less distance from work, and not just geographically. Neither Kate nor Ellie was home yet. She found Derek enjoying a beer after his day in court. Jordan was uncomfortably reminded of Valerie's words, and the fact that she was going to see her more often. Perhaps, at some point, she had to come clean and tell Ellie the whole story. Then again, Ellie was and had always been more oriented towards the future. She might be okay not knowing all about Jordan's past mistakes. At the very least, she could guess.

Derek took another beer from the fridge and handed it to her.

"Okay, shoot. What did I miss?"

"Maria made an arrest. If we're lucky, we can put the Ashcroft case to rest as well."

She cringed at the thought.

"Good for her," he said, his voice level. "You don't seem too happy about it. Why is it not the big deal it should be?"

"I don't know. If she has a good public defender, I'm afraid the case is going to fall apart. Maybe I'm afraid it's not."

"Why? You don't believe she did it?"

"It's all too easy. Maybe someone made an effort to make it that easy for us."

"It fits though, the evidence against her, her behavior at the bar, and access to the heart medication. You think someone framed her?" Derek asked incredulously.

"I know it, but I can't prove it. Come on, when do we ever have evidence fall into our laps like this?"

"It happens."

"Yeah. I'm not sure it happened in this case. Are we even paying for this?" she asked, pointing to the bottle. "I'm starting to feel like we're taking advantage."

Derek considered the question for much longer than he needed to, in Jordan's opinion, which told her he wasn't just thinking about the meals and drinks they'd had here lately.

"Maria is doing okay." It sounded like a question.

"She is. She's still a bit pissed at you, but she'll get over it. Look, I didn't mean to judge. I know it's already late to say that, but this is between you and McCarthy. I get it. Do you know where this is going?"

He laughed. "Didn't you just say this was between me and Kate?"

"I'm your partner. I still get to ask the nosy questions."

"To be honest? I don't know. This, for now, it works for both of us. She doesn't seem to want more at this point, so that's how it's going to be. Are we going to talk about you and Harding?"

"We had the perfect vacation together. What else do you want to know?"

"You're going to keep the house in the woods?"

"It's not exactly 'in the woods,' and yes, I plan to keep it. I love living there. It's not like it's haunted or anything."

"So, you plan on asking her to come live with you at some point?"

For sure, it didn't take a detective to identify the elephant in the room.

"We're not there yet," she said, got up and used a magnet to stick a twenty on the fridge, before she took out another couple of beers. "Pizza is going to be on you, if they ever get here."

"All right, I get you. Is your mother still bothering you?"

"Not at the moment. Can we talk politics or the weather now?"

They both laughed. Jordan was grateful that she had managed to repair friendships on the verge of breaking, but she couldn't deny Derek had brought up some uncomfortable subjects. Finally, they heard the key in the lock. Kate and Ellie were home.

❦

"I don't know what the problem is. Life is good. There was an arrest, finally, which makes the lieutenant happy. I have a feeling...but that's not it. I could be wrong. We might have found the person to tie it all together."

"Somehow I don't believe that's giving you sleepless nights," Dr. Burns concluded correctly.

"No." Jordan sighed and turned from where she was standing by the window, to the psychiatrist. "I set the date with Kathryn. Now I'm worried she might actually want to do this, reconciliation, redemption, whatever. And I'm worried she won't show up, which is ridiculous. This is what I know of her—not showing up. It's the most likely scenario."

"And what if she does?"

"It's why I asked her to come to my house instead of going to a public place. She might be asking for absolution, all tearful, and if there were other people around, I wouldn't have much of a choice, would I?"

"You feel pressured?"

"Wouldn't you?"

"I can't speak for your birthmother," Dr. Burns said, "but whatever the plan is, this is something she obviously needs to do for herself, whatever the outcome. You need to figure out the part that is for you, what will help *you* move on."

"I know what you're going to say. Forgiveness is not for the other person, it's for you, and it's vital in order to let go. I lived with a psychiatrist for a long time. I picked up some of the lines."

If Dr. Burns was offended by this assessment of her profession, she didn't mention it.

"Well, we don't all have the same lines all the time. In my opinion, we don't always have to forgive, not even our parents. The letting go only works if it's really right for you. It is up to you, you know."

"Would that make me a terrible person? To hold on to my side of the story for so long?"

"Of course not. Whatever you'll hear, it doesn't mean what you thought and felt, or what you're feeling right now, is any less valid."

It sounded logical. It wouldn't be easy to remember it.

"Thank you," she said. "I really needed to hear that."

⁓

Ellie stood in front of the full-length mirror, tugging at her dress. She was aware of Jordan standing in the doorway, regarding her with a smile.

"What? It's a high society party. We don't get invited to these things all the time, so we should at least dress in style. From what I read, it's a pretty promising project."

She could see the surprise in Jordan's expression. "I read up on Abigail's competition a bit, and apparently this new mascara will be affordable, environmentally friendly, and it will make you look glamorous. It looks like some people are already bashing it, because they're afraid she could take too big a piece of the cake."

Jordan came up behind her and kissed her neck softly. While Ellie thought she was gorgeous in the white shirt and skinny jeans, she was not appropriately dressed for the occasion.

"What would I do without you? I know as much about these things as poor Mr. Ashcroft did."

Ellie laughed. "Poor thing. Yes, that's what you have me for. I give you another tip. You should get dressed now, or we'll be late."

"I am dressed." Jordan sighed. "All right. I don't think I have anything that..."

"Or should I help you?"

Ellie began to unbutton Jordan's shirt, her fingers touching soft, warm skin, until Jordan stilled her hands.

"If you do, we're definitely going to be late. Okay. That dress must still be in the back of the closet."

"I'm surprised you didn't put it in the attic," Ellie said wryly. "Come on, this is going to be fun."

"It's not just for fun."

"I know. That doesn't mean we can't snark afterwards about the rich and famous...Is there going to be anybody famous?"

"I have no idea. Okay. Wait for me here."

Despite Jordan's grumbling, Ellie thought she looked fabulous in the simple black dress and pumps. She was also aware that this was a rare occasion, because Jordan was already complaining about the two-inch heels.

"I don't know how you do it."

"Practice makes perfect in everything."

"Right. That's not something I care to practice further. Are we ready?"

"What? No. Let me do your hair? I'm aware this is not just a social occasion, but the Ashcrofts don't have to be reminded, right? If they're comfortable, maybe that will help us."

Jordan still looked doubtful. Apparently, she had failed to consider everything this event entailed. "You know I only put up with all of this, because I love you?"

For a glorious moment, nothing else mattered, then Ellie had to remind herself that they were still on a tight timetable.

"I love you too. Now relax."

Mrs. Santos had taken care of the catering, but she didn't look happy about it. Ellie knew there was no evidence to tie her to either of the murders, but the arrest of her niece had to hit her hard. It was difficult to tell if the siblings were kind or cruel by letting her be a visible part of this event. Some of the guests were clearly talking about subjects other than mascara.

Abigail Ashcroft had set up a space in the grand entrance hall where the carpet had finally been installed on the stairs. Ellie noticed the flash of disgust in Jordan's expression. This had been a crime scene not so long ago, now there were busy waiters handing out champagne and canapés, and well-dressed people standing around in clusters, waiting for the big event. Huge banners with a model sporting the new improved cosmetics greeted the guests. The woman in question was nowhere to be seen, but Craig Ashcroft spotted them and came over.

"Detective, I'm so glad you could make it." His gaze went to Ellie, and a pause ensued as he obviously tried to remember where he'd seen her before.

"Officer Harding," she said. "We met at the station."

"Oh, that's true. Welcome. I hope you can forget about work for a while. Abby has something amazing prepared." He smiled at Jordan, and Ellie almost expected a wink. "If you'll excuse me. Enjoy...and don't forget your free samples. Abby will find you later to say hello."

"What was that?" Ellie asked, amused, when he was out of earshot. "The last time I saw him, he wasn't all that friendly."

"When he brought that invitation, he apologized for wanting to sue the department, as originally planned...and he suggested we're family. I'm not sure I agree with all of those additions to my 'family' lately."

"How about this one?" Ellie said and kissed her cheek quickly.

Jordan smiled as she accepted a glass of champagne from a waiter. "This one is perfect."

Chapter Eleven

"**I** know my father would be so proud if he could see this. Thank you all for sharing this special moment with me. This is for you, Dad." Abby ended her speech in tears, earning thunderous applause from the crowd.

Craig was clapping too, standing behind to the left. The daughter was there, wearing a princess dress and a tiara, her nanny in tow.

The champagne was outrageously good, not something Jordan could afford on a regular basis. Still, she felt slightly nauseated at the show they were witnessing. On the other occasions she'd come into this house, it had been a very different atmosphere, and part of it was lingering. Gerald Ashcroft had been murdered right here. She assumed that the interest of many guests wasn't so much in Abby's mascara, but more of a sensationalistic nature. Her feet hurt. Ellie, on the other hand, had no problem balancing on her stiletto heels.

Her cell phone was vibrating in the purse Ellie had made her wear. Jordan found a quieter corner to take a look, suppressing a sigh when she saw whom it was from.

I'm at the hospital. I'm so sorry, but I don't know if I can make it. If you want to see me... Jordan put the phone back into the purse.

She couldn't get drunk at this party, but nobody could stop her once they were out of here and off-duty.

She went back to the general party area, noticing that Linwood Ashcroft was not attending his sister's big event. Jordan thought it would be odd to discover that the two of them had something in common after all, finding it a bit problematic to launch Abigail's business only days after her father's funeral, in the place where he had died.

Her tears had seemed to be genuine.

"Detective Carpenter, I hope you're enjoying yourself."

Abigail Ashcroft shook her hand. "Craig told me you brought your partner. I'm so glad we all meet again for a happier occasion...now that the murderer is finally caught."

"Ms. Santos hasn't been convicted yet," Jordan reminded her.

"But you wouldn't arrest her if she was innocent, right? What a cunning little bitch, pardon my language. I think she weaseled her way in and got a lot of money out of my father, because he liked her aunt." She sighed dramatically. "At least, that stops now."

"Ellie told me you have a great product on your hands. It looks like the investment Craig made worked out."

"Oh, yes. He has more of a vision than Dad has—had, I mean." Abigail's solemn moment didn't last long. "But that's not so much of a surprise, is it, him being gay."

Jordan tried hard not to cringe. Being gay hardly had anything to do with that. It was odd and sad at the same time when the younger generation in a family was becoming more close-minded. With a pang of guilt, she remembered Kathryn's message. Was she making the same mistakes?

No, you couldn't compare years of neglect to a parent trying not to spoil their children out of their highly privileged minds.

She would stop by the hospital in the morning, just to make sure she had nothing to feel guilty about.

"Linwood isn't here tonight?"

Abby laughed, but it sounded bitter. "Linnie, he doesn't have much of a vision about anything. He's still cranky Dad didn't just let him take over. It looks like we'll all have to work a bit more for this money."

"Maybe that was the vision your dad had. For all of you to work together."

Abby smiled brightly. "I guess that one came true. Please, don't forget your swag later."

"Of course not."

That got her a curious look from Abby, but she obviously decided Jordan was serious. "Great. I'll sneak you an extra basket. Maybe you have some colleagues or girlfriends who might be interested." She giggled. "I hope it's okay to say that. I didn't mean..."

"It's all right. I appreciate your generosity."

"You're welcome. If only Dad was here. He could see he was wrong about so many things."

It occurred to Jordan that even with Aleja Santos accused of murder, Abigail Ashcroft was still jealous of her.

⁂

"We can go by the hospital later," Ellie offered.

"I prefer not to. She might misinterpret that."

"Don't you want to know?"

Jordan sighed. "I want to go back to a time when she wasn't my responsibility."

"That's not what it's about. You'll feel better."

"I guess."

She wasn't completely unselfish in this either, Ellie realized. She sympathized, deeply. Jordan had every right to be suspicious of Kathryn's motives, and yet, Ellie's efforts came from a place where she wished her parents were still alive. There were so many things she didn't have the chance to tell them, to share with them, but with their relationship intact, those regrets were on a different scale. She wanted Jordan to have that chance, clear things up while she still could.

Ellie was already afraid of what they could find out, with Kathryn's many attempts to reconnect, and the sudden hospital stay. From what she knew about her, it was more than likely that she suffered health problems.

She didn't know what the right thing was in this situation—all she knew was that they needed, deserved some peace that lasted a little longer than a couple of weeks of vacation.

Before she could think about a way to voice all of those concerns, the room was plunged into sudden darkness. Ellie instinctively reached out for Jordan, and then, there was a scream. More screams and frantic footsteps followed.

"Stay right here by the staircase," Jordan said. "I'll try to find a flashlight. I'm sure Mrs. Santos has one."

Ellie reluctantly let go, holding on to the staircase. The place hadn't seemed so crowded at first, but now that people were running in all directions in panicked moves, the room felt claustrophobic, the darkness adding a suffocating atmosphere that plunged her right back into the dark apartment where Danny Roth had held her. She had pleaded with him and was still fairly certain she could have succeeded, if it wasn't for the company he kept. Roth had hired Josh Ward to attack her so he could play the hero, and when that didn't work out, he took her from her apartment. Roth had his favorite delusions, Ward was simply...cruel. It was a small piece of metal, and Roth returning to the apartment that had saved her, given her an opportunity to avoid much worse.

The light came on, and she realized she was trembling. The front doors were wide open, but people had stopped running. Most of them were standing in a wide circle near one of the majestic windows, where Jordan had earlier checked her cell phone. There was a figure lying on the floor.

Abigail Ashcroft was moaning in pain, the crimson stain near the waist of her pristine white dress spreading, the knife still lying next to her.

The sight jolted her into action, and she ran over to the small group. Jordan was kneeling next to the woman, applying pressure to the wound with a towel. Without words, Ellie took over while Jordan made the necessary calls.

The guests weren't leaving any longer but studying the scene with fascination.

"Get back," Jordan directed. "Mrs. Santos, is there a list of all guests? I need everyone to stay right here."

The housekeeper nodded, regarding Abby with a frightened expression. "She's going to make it, right?"

"Of course, don't worry. The wound isn't that deep. Please make sure that everyone stays right here." Nevertheless, her hands were red with blood, the sight making Ellie shudder.

"We have to wait for backup, then we have to shake this place upside down," Jordan muttered under her breath, only for Ellie to hear. "Whoever did this is probably still in the house."

Ellie nodded. It was a chilling, yet likely conclusion. This night was going to be a lot longer than anyone had expected.

Chapter Twelve

H enderson and Waters arrived minutes later, with a group of uniformed officers. Libby was one of them.

"Hey there," Jordan said. "I need someone to go to the hospital with Abigail Ashcroft, see if she remembers anything. She was pretty out of it earlier, but there might be something once she gets over the shock. Maybe someone threatened her prior to this event."

"I'll go," Waters offered.

"All right. Mrs. Santos helped set up a few rooms upstairs. We'll have to go over this with every one of these ladies and gentlemen."

"That is unacceptable," a man in his early forties said indignantly. "We'll have to pay the babysitter service extra."

Just a look at his suit told Ellie that he probably could afford infinite hours of babysitter service, and then she nearly did a double take when she recognized him.

Jordan got up and walked over to him. "I'm sorry for the inconvenience, Mr...?"

Ouch. He didn't seem all that fazed about Jordan's lack of recognition, though. He all but shrank back at the sight of the blood on her hands.

"Bond," he scoffed. "You can't keep us here. What if that person decides to attack someone else?"

"That's highly unlikely—"

"That's not good enough for me! You'll hear from my lawyer!"

"Whatever suits you, Mr. Bond. If you'll excuse me now. We have to talk to all the guests. The sooner we get started, the sooner you can all return home."

He clearly wasn't placated. Ellie wondered what possessed all these rich people to threaten to sue all the time. Was it their way of setting them and their needs apart from others', claiming they were more important? They would have to interview all the guests, no matter whose party this was, and how much money they had.

Jordan turned to her, her expression conveying her frustration clearly. "I need to go wash my hands," she said. "You can join the others."

"I will, but let me get you some clothes from the car first."

Ellie didn't wait for an answer but made her way through the crowd of grumbling guests outside, and to where they had parked earlier. Since they were still practically living together, but not in the same house, a lot of foresight and planning was involved. Jordan had only reluctantly agreed to the implied dress code, so she'd be happy to be done with it, especially with the blood on her dress.

She found her in one of the downstairs guest bathrooms. "Here," she said, handing her the bag with a change of clothes.

"Thank you. Not you?" Jordan asked while she reached behind her to pull down the zipper, cursing when it got stuck. Ellie stepped in. "Just the shoes. I'm fine otherwise. No, now's not the time to gloat."

"Tell me about it." Jordan breathed a sigh of relief when she had changed dress and heels for jeans, shirt and a pair of sneakers. "Let's go find the rest of the crew."

"Jordan, wait a second. You know that was Congressman Bond?"

"Oh crap. That's why he looked familiar."

"Yeah, one of those who'd love to vote yes on repealing marriage equality. Okay. I just meant we have to..."

"Please don't say, tread carefully, okay?"

Ellie shook her head with a smile.

Derek joined them on the way down to the cellar of the Ashcroft house. Fortunately, they had Mrs. Santos to show them the utility room. Ellie guessed that someone had manipulated the breaker, so that meant...two suspects? She knew that Jordan still suspected the siblings in the Ashcroft murder, but the brothers didn't see eye to eye either, so why would they turn on Abigail?

In any case, they could say for certain that Aleja Santos didn't have anything to do with this. As they walked deeper into the room, the now familiar, unsettling feeling crept up on her. Dark spaces. They didn't seem to freak Jordan out.

"Do you really think someone from the outside did this?" Derek asked.

Jordan shook her head. "This was someone who knew the place, and how long it would take to get away. I'm not sure that we'll find prints on those breakers. They're smarter than that."

"I know who you are thinking of, but if it's the breakers, someone has to have been down here while the other one attacked Abigail. If not, it took skills to set this up, more than I think either of them has."

"Money buys you that."

"Risky. More witnesses."

"Money buys discretion as well, but I'd still go with the breaker theory. And at this point...I'm not sure who would want to harm her. Craig was the one who helped her get to their father's money."

The back and forth between Jordan and Derek was a welcome distraction for Ellie who felt that the air was getting thin.

"We're okay down here?" she asked.

"You can go," Henderson assured her. "Let us know if there's anything from the guests yet."

"Okay." Ellie took a deep breath, prompting a concerned look from Jordan. "Are you okay?"

"Yes, just a little...it's hot down here. I'll see you upstairs."

"Yeah."

Ellie saw Jordan examine the wall around the breakers with gloved hands before she turned to go upstairs. A pained curse made her spin around, and the sight made her stomach churn. She almost fainted, even though Jordan would be the more likely candidate, with blood dripping from her hand. Again. This time, it was hers, from a cut across her palm.

"Damn it," she said, and found a couple of other choice words. "What the hell is this?"

Underneath the cabinet ran an almost invisible, razor-sharp wire. Ellie stared, mesmerized, until Derek snapped at her. "Are you just going to stand there?"

"Hey. Derek. Cut it out. I'm not dying." Jordan opened the door to a closet, but of course there was nothing to cover up the wound. "Let's all go upstairs now. I think I've seen enough."

Her words jolted Ellie into action, and she hurried upstairs to find Mrs. Santos and a clean bandage, not necessarily in that order.

Predictably, none of the guests had heard or seen anything out of the ordinary, but a number of them doubted that the police had a right to question them.

"There's nothing much you can do here right now," Derek said. "This might need stitches. Let Ellie drive you to the hospital."

Jordan wished she had something to argue with, but she couldn't come up with much. "I could check in on Ms. Ashcroft. Waters hasn't called yet?"

"No. You do that, but make sure you see a doctor for yourself first."

"It's a scratch," she said, wincing as the wound pulsed angrily. The blood was already coming through the bandage Mrs. Santos had provided for her.

"Yeah, whatever. Harding, make sure she sees that doctor."

"Will do," Ellie said, looking pale still, but determined. "Let's go."

Jordan had another reason to give in. Having some alone time with Ellie during the drive gave her the chance to ask some questions that had been on her mind since before the unfortunate encounter with the razor wire. She wasn't going to waste any time either.

"What happened down there?"

"What do you mean? You should know."

"I mean...you. We didn't have that much to drink. Are you coming down with something?"

"No. I don't think so." Ellie sighed but didn't offer up any more information.

"But...?"

"No but. I got a little queasy, that's all. Then it got worse. It's not like the sight of blood makes me sick. I just hate to see you get hurt."

"Ellie," Jordan said softly.

"All right, you asked for it. Dark places, you know? Cellars, apartments, all that, I thought it was way behind me, but it's still...It's hard sometimes. I'll get over it."

"I know. You can talk to me."

"Yeah. It's just...It's nothing really, and you already have so much on your plate. I don't want to add to that."

"You don't. It's not always about me."

Ellie smiled when Jordan took her hand at a red light. "Talking things through isn't your favorite thing. I mean...I get where that is coming from."

"I can do better. Now let's see if we can get Ms. Ashcroft to talk. I really hope stitches is not the only thing I'll get out of this."

She had to do better indeed. Jordan of all people shouldn't have missed the signs, considering her own intimate knowledge of dark spaces.

"They didn't say a word. I didn't even realize what was happening until I felt the pain. I managed to pull out the knife, but I must have fainted from the shock."

Indeed, the depth of the wound indicated that the perpetrator either didn't have enough time, or they didn't mean to kill Abigail in the first place.

Abigail Ashcroft cast them a look that was more irritated than frightened. "I told all of that to Detective Waters. Now please, leave me alone for a few hours, before I have to pick up what's left of my business."

"In case you remember anything else..."

"Believe me, I know where to find you."

"Thank you." With the way this night had turned out, Jordan had no intention of dragging this out any longer than it needed to be. She would have loved to head straight home, but of course Ellie would have none of it. At least, they were in a quiet area where the ER doctor was able to see her not much later.

118

"Have you gotten all your shots?" Ellie wondered out loud.

"Seriously?" Apparently, that wasn't the right answer, because Ellie frowned. "Yes, I'm up to date, but I really want to go home. This is a waste of time."

The doctor who examined the cut a few minutes later, didn't think so, and Jordan resigned to the fact that going home was not in the immediate future. Other cases that were more of an emergency than hers required the staff's attention, prolonging the wait until she could get the necessary sutures done.

She breathed a sigh of relief when they finally left the hospital a couple of hours later. However, she'd known Ellie would bring up a certain subject once more.

"We could check on Kathryn quickly," she said. "It's not far from here. We could have breakfast after..."

"I'd rather lie down for a bit before I go back in." Jordan sat up straighter in her seat when Ellie took the exit anyway. "Um...did you not hear what I just said?"

"Yes, I heard you clearly. You said we were going to talk, so let's talk. We don't know anything at all, why she's in the hospital. If she's sick, you'll want to know. If there's something you need to say, you should say it, if only for your own peace of mind. Believe me, I know what I'm talking about."

"I don't doubt that, but...It's not the same. I've said everything. I know I said I'd listen to her side, excuses, no doubt, but she's the one who said she might not make it. I don't want us to fight. Not over this."

"Trust me?" It was hard to deny Ellie anything, especially when she turned that pleading gaze on Jordan.

"Eyes on the road," Jordan muttered. "Yes, of course I trust you."

"You go in there for a few minutes, and then we'll leave. I promise."

"The things I do for you."

"Because you love me?" Ellie said with a smile, but she kept her gaze on the street ahead.

"Among other things. All right. Let's see what she has to say."

Even though she'd seen her just days ago, Kathryn seemed aged. She sat up, a tired smile on her face when Jordan entered the room.

"You came. That's nice of you."

"I don't have much time."

Ellie had come with her but stayed at a respectful distance as Jordan hesitantly approached the bed. Kathryn reached for her hand, holding it in both of hers.

"What happened to you?"

"Nothing." Jordan retrieved her hand quickly, finding the brief contact unsettling. "I was going to ask you that question though. Will you be able to come, or not?"

"I don't know yet. They're still running some tests."

Jordan bit her lip, afraid of what she might say. It wasn't much of a stretch to assume Kathryn wasn't in perfect health, considering the ways she had abused her body. The fact that they were keeping her here was troubling. She doubted that most hospitals would keep patients who could hardly afford the care, when there was nothing wrong.

"Okay. I hope you're going to be all right, and that I can still see you next Saturday."

"Could you...stay for a bit?"

"I'm really busy right now. We spent most of the night at a crime scene. Sorry."

Kathryn nodded. "I understand." She cast a hesitant smile at Ellie before looking back at Jordan. "Apparently, the numbers are all messed up. I guess once they find the reason, they'll put me on some medication I can't afford to begin with. I won-der—"

She didn't finish the sentence when the door opened, and Jim Larson entered the room, his surprise showing. "Jordan."

The room felt claustrophobic to Jordan all of a sudden. A few months ago, she would have been fine never seeing either of them again, at least that's what she had believed for many years. The choice hadn't been hers, but she could make a choice now.

"We were just leaving," she said, and this time, Ellie didn't protest.

Chapter Thirteen

They had managed to go to Ellie's for a few hours of sleep—not enough—and a quick breakfast on the go. There was no time to even start to process Kathryn's hospitalization, and what it might mean.

On her desk, Jordan found a gift basket with best wishes from Ashcroft Cosmetics.

"Ellie got one of those too," Kate McCarthy remarked a tad too cheerfully. "How's the hand?"

"I'll survive. You have anything for me?"

Kate put the stack of folders she was carrying, on Jordan's desk and opened the first one.

"Wait, that's not it. The statements from last night? There was something interesting. Apparently, somebody got booted from the guest list, and they weren't too happy about it. Looks like cosmetics is a real cutthroat business."

"Well, we're lucky no one's throat got cut," Jordan remarked. "You want that basket?"

"I do," Libby Marshall said from behind Kate. "Forget about it. I was kidding," she hurried to add when Jordan didn't answer. She couldn't care less who took the basket. A photo in the file Kate had left open on her desk, caught Jordan's attention.

"Wait. Who's that guy?"

"Raphael Deane. Why, do you know him?"

"Who is he?"

"The only trace in the Beaumont case," Kate explained. "The mother who came in on the day you were back from vacation? Someone saw her getting into a car with him, but now they have both vanished. His last known address is abandoned, neighbors know nothing about him or where he might have gone."

"Okay."

"That's it?" Kate sounded surprised.

"I don't know. He looks familiar. I'll let you know when I figure it out, and by all means, take that basket. Share it. I mean it. No, seriously." Jordan pushed the basket towards Kate and Libby. They went back to their work, taking back files and Abby Ashcroft's gift with them. Jordan sighed in relief. The moment of peace didn't last long.

"Handing out gifts to other women?" she heard a familiar voice ask. "What is your girlfriend going to say about that?"

"She has one of her own. Hey, Val. Do you have a reason to be here?"

"I do. I want you to be in court for Aleja Santos' arraignment."

"Why? They're just going to set bail."

"Yeah, that's what I'm trying to avoid," the A.D.A. said. "Santos isn't poor, and her aunt just inherited a sizable amount of money. There's a flight risk. I need you to testify to what you saw. It speaks to her state of mind, and that she might be a danger to others."

"Come on. She would be crazy to run, now that we had another murder attempt related to the Ashcrofts."

"I've seen crazier things," Valerie said. "Tomorrow at eight. Be on time, I'll buy you a coffee afterwards. Thank you."

"You don't have to..."

Valerie had already left. Nobody seemed to bother to listen to her today...Although, if Jordan was honest, Ellie was probably the only one with no ulterior motives.

The encounter with Kathryn had told her everything and nothing. She'd still have to wait and see if that conversation was going to happen after all. Meanwhile she had a full day ahead.

She skipped her lunch break in favor of a visit neither the lieutenant nor Valerie would approve of. Jordan knew she had to try once more before Aleja lost all trust in the authorities and shut down. The consequences would only get worse.

She didn't believe that Aleja was responsible for two murders. Maybe she didn't want her success with Darla to be marred by the memory of a young woman she had let down—most of all, Jordan knew that the confrontation with her own past left her with a chilling image of what could have been. She could have run away, ended up on the streets like Darla. Harbored that anger and get caught up in the system like Aleja now was. If she had anything to offer that would change the direction, Jordan would.

When Aleja saw her, she shook her head.

"What are you doing here?"

"I don't have much time. I wanted to talk to you."

"About what? You all made up your mind, didn't you? With all the things they found in the storage unit, I'm done for. I'm not even so handy that I would need all that stuff." She laughed bitterly. "So much for the lesbian card, huh?"

"Focus for a moment, please. The A.D.A. wants me to testify about what happened in the bar."

Jordan didn't like the resignation in Aleja's expression. "That's bad, I assume."

"It's not good. Aleja, I need you to work with me here. If someone set you up, they most likely did so for a reason. I

125

want you to think hard. Is there anyone you got in a fight with, anything that you can remember?"

"My lawyer asked the same question. I don't know! Hell, I was just doing my job, going out for a drink every once in a while, and visiting my aunt when I could. Craig sometimes drove me home. We talked. His brother was giving him a hard time after he'd married into that ultra-conservative family. People suck, don't they? If you can't stand up for your own family, what kind of person does that make you?"

"You would stand up for yours, that's for sure. You care a great deal about your aunt."

"Please. She adored him. Besides, she didn't even know about Sandra. At first, I thought it was some random guy, but maybe she knew him, and that's why she went with him in the first place? Maybe I know him too, I have no idea! She didn't tell me a whole lot about herself. That wasn't the point, as you can imagine. I think she worked as a beautician or something. In any case, she was good with her make-up."

"That's something," Jordan said, even though it wasn't a whole lot. As far as she knew, Sandra had been unemployed at the time of her death, though her financial records showed some money coming in. The source was yet unclear. "I'll see you tomorrow in court. Hang in there."

Aleja gave her a wry smile. "And why do you care?"

"Somebody should, don't you think?"

<hr/>

"Where have you been?" Derek asked when she finally got to see three missed calls and called him back. "We have something interesting here. Danielle d'Amour, the woman who was uninvited from Ashcroft's launch party?"

"That's her real name?"

"Yes, but that's beside the point. Her firm is quite a bit bigger than Ashcroft's, and they merged with a pharma company last year. Guess what? That company produces the same heart medication as Aleja's employer."

"That doesn't prove anything, but at least it could generate some doubt?"

"Well, I don't know about that. Aleja worked with them...and so did Sandra Paulson at some point. D'Amour says she fired Paulson months ago and was so busy she didn't watch the news, so she didn't come forward. The point is, Aleja probably knew Sandra before they hooked up that night."

"So she lied to me. Shit."

"She lied to you...when? Jordan, when did you talk to her?"

"I'll tell you later. Meet me in twenty, so we can sort all of this out. Doss and Waters are around somewhere?"

"I'll find them. See you." Jordan pressed End Call and then hit the steering wheel for good measure, the resulting pain an unmistakable reminder of last night's misfortune.

She arrived at the same time as Ellie and Casey who had a charge in the back of their car.

"Busy day?" Jordan commented, earning a glare from the young man they had arrested.

"Tried to steal a car in broad daylight," Casey told her. "He didn't get far from there. Ellie's got some mad driving skills."

"I don't doubt that."

"Do you have a moment?" Ellie asked. "We have to get him to booking, but after that..."

"Sure. Come find me at my desk."

As Jordan took the elevator to her floor, she had to admit that for the first time, she had doubts about Aleja. She might have been wrong, but at least there was still the question of motive.

127

Had someone influenced her? Jordan was still reluctant to believe the young woman could have planned both murders from the start and executed them.

People did the strangest things for love.

❧

"I'm really sorry." They had retreated to the break room for a coffee and a shared chocolate bar, and Ellie could finally express what had bothered her the whole day. "I shouldn't have made you see Kathryn. It's your decision. I shouldn't have acted like I did."

Jordan seemed surprised at her apology. "To tell you the truth, I didn't think all that much about it, but it's okay. You were right. It doesn't mean all is well, but if I don't have that conversation now, it might be something I regret later."

"It might help you too. There are so many questions I still have, that will never be answered." Ellie sighed. "That's a conversation for another time and place. I just wanted to make sure you know I'm not trying to make your life any more complicated."

"Don't worry. My life would be a lot more complicated if it weren't for you."

Jordan cast a quick look at the still closed door and kissed Ellie. "My house tonight? I need to go to court tomorrow. We could order in..."

"Hey, Jordan, here's—"

Derek didn't get any further before A.D.A. Esposito stormed into the room.

"That's just great, exactly the Jordan Carpenter I remember. Rules are for other people, and every means justifies the end. Are you out of your mind?"

Jordan leaned against the vending machine, giving the other woman an amused glance.

"Hey. Stop. I'm sorry, and I already know I might be wrong about Santos. No need to yell."

Ellie observed the exchange, intrigued.

"You practically told her you're on her side, because, apparently, everyone except Detective of the year Carpenter got it wrong. Forget about the evidence, if you have the gut feeling that she's innocent, then she must be, right?"

Henderson's gaze said *I'm sorry, I can't help you*. However, he lingered, just as interested as Ellie who, unfortunately, didn't have any more of a reason to stay here.

"I better go," she mumbled and moved to leave.

"No, wait a second!" Jordan said, holding her back with a hand on her arm. "There's something we need to talk about."

"Unbelievable," Esposito muttered. "Detective, this conversation isn't over!"

"Ellie, do you know anything about Rhonda's recent ex? The guy?" Jordan asked, ignoring the A.D.A.

This was too much of a non-sequitur even for Ellie.

"I never met him, but I'm sure you have a reason to ask me this?"

"I sure do. Come on, I have to tell McCarthy. He is connected to the missing woman. They will want to go see Rhonda."

"Okay. Slow down. Tell me."

Henderson shrugged and went back to his desk.

"Don't screw up tomorrow," Esposito warned and left as well.

"Okay, that worked well. So, what is it with Rhonda?" Ellie's eyes widened. "You didn't just say that to get Esposito off your back?"

Jordan winced at the metaphor. "No, I didn't. I swear. When we were looking for you...I went to see Rhonda, at work, and once outside her apartment building. There was a guy, he seemed obnoxious, but she claimed he wasn't threatening her."

"I talked to her once to say I was okay, but that's all. Frankly, I have no idea what you're talking about."

"The missing woman, Jennifer Beaumont? She was last seen with this guy. Maybe Rhonda can help us find him."

"Okay. I see." Ellie wasn't too eager to see Rhonda again. However, they'd had a polite phone conversation after her abduction, so there was a chance it wouldn't been painful.

Besides, she knew that Kate was invested in this case. Finding Jennifer Beaumont would do her a lot of good, both personally and for her career.

"I'll call Kate. Maybe Rhonda can come in."

Chapter Fourteen

R honda had asked a colleague to take over for her and came to the station right away. She seemed a bit perplexed at the request as they retreated to an interview room with Ellie, Kate, and the Missing Persons detective. Rogers was in his fifties. Ellie had only seen him a few times before, but Kate had worked closely with him on this case. She looked excited.

"Hey, it's nice to see you again, Ellie," Rhonda said. "What is this all about? Raphael got himself in trouble? I'm not surprised."

"Why is that, Ms. Marks?" Rogers asked.

"Well, there's a reason he's my ex. He seemed okay at first, saying all the right things, but it got weird from there."

"Weird how, Rhonda?" Kate pushed. "Do you know where he is now? That's all we need to know."

"First of all, no, I don't know where he is. He talked about having family in Iowa, maybe he went back there. As for the weirdness, he started telling me how to dress, how to wear my hair, and so on. At first it was like, it's really pretty that way, and soon we got to, not like that, it makes you look real slutty."

Ellie thought with a shudder that she'd become blonde because Rhonda liked it that way, but she got a different vibe from Deane.

"In any case, I wasn't going to put up with that crap any longer, and I broke up with him. He came to see me a couple of times, tried to change my mind…That's when the detective came looking for you, Ellie. She offered me to file a restraining order, but I said no. I didn't think he was that dangerous, and he vanished shortly after that. We met through a couple of friends we had in common, but they haven't seen him either."

"Can you give us their names?"

"Sure. Ellen and Dwayne. I have their addresses if you want them."

"That's great, thank you," Ellie said. "If you see him, please give us a call. It's important."

"You're not going to tell me what he did?" Rhonda's eyes widened dramatically. "He didn't kill anyone, did he?"

"We assume that he'll be able to help us with an ongoing investigation. That will be all, Ms. Marks. Thank you." Rogers rose, picking up the notepad with the addresses Rhonda had written on it. Kate followed him out of the room, which gave Ellie and Rhonda a sudden and awkward privacy.

"I'm really glad you're okay," Rhonda said softly, as she stepped closer. She reached out to tuck a strand of hair that had escaped the neat bun, behind Ellie's ear. "You're still blonde."

Ellie took a step backwards. "Yeah. My girlfriend likes it that way."

"Touché." Rhonda laughed. "Look. I didn't mean anything. I just want you to know I met Raph long after we broke up."

"You mean after you vanished into nowhere."

"Same difference. And I didn't exactly vanish. I've had the same job for the past ten years. Doesn't matter now. You're happy, I'm happy. Maybe you'd like to get a coffee sometime, and we can catch up?"

"I'm not sure that's a good idea."

"Maybe not, but I'm curious." Rhonda winked as she picked up her purse. "I hope you'll come by the store. You'll love the new collection, I promise you. I can find my way out."

She kissed Ellie on the cheek and left.

Closing the door behind her, Ellie thought that the idea of staying friends with the ex was nothing but a delusion. That coffee—or shopping trip, for that matter—was never going to happen. She was glad though that they could do something to help Kate's case move forward. She was a lot more focused, seemed less lost than she had after her fiancé's death.

⁂

"Do you like my hair the way it is?"

"I like everything about you the way it is," Jordan confirmed as she ran her fingers lazily through the blonde strands. Waking up far before the alarm had its advantages.

"Sorry, that was silly." Ellie sighed. "What is it with exes always sticking around? No, you don't have to answer that. I don't even know why I'm still thinking about it."

"How did it go...otherwise?"

"She had some names. They might help find the guy. It's not her, really. I'm still angry at myself that I made so many changes. It wasn't until...That night I realized life is damn short. You have to take any chance you get."

Jordan pulled her close, thinking ruefully that she'd have to get up in five minutes or less. "I'm glad I fit somewhere in that equation."

"Me too. I heard someone called me a self-entitled twit for that, but it's—"

"What? Who did that?"

"It's not important," Ellie insisted. "There was some talk, as I'm sure you're aware of, but it wasn't worse than what Kate had to deal with. It's the same immature clique of guys being twelve-year-old boys. First, they told her how sorry they were about Jensen, then not much later they called her a slut. You know how it is. You can get out of high school, but you can't get high school out of some people."

Despite herself, Jordan had to laugh. "That's good. I'd still like to know who. For future reference."

"You have to get up now. If you're late, Esposito will have your hide."

"Yeah, whatever. Give me a name."

"Okay." Ellie sighed, "Chris Atwood. Don't do or say anything, please. Hell, I'm sure he forgot about it by now."

"What you, or Kate, do in your private lives is none of their business. This is unacceptable." Jordan finally got out of bed and started gathering her clothes. "Someone should tell Bristol. I'm sure that's not the kind of work environment he wants for his precinct." Jordan was aware, but she had done her best to ignore the gossip at work, after Darby, and after she and everyone else learned that TJ Pratt was her biological father. People talked. That didn't mean they were entitled to harassment.

"Let it go. Please? They've been quiet lately. I really don't want them to feel that important."

"Okay. I'll keep that in mind, but only because you are right about Esposito. I hope it's going to be quick."

"If it's not, I'll come by at lunchtime," Ellie offered. "Now get into the shower, or do I have to join you?"

"Promises," Jordan muttered.

Moments later, they stood entwined under the shower spray, and it took every bit of self-restraint not to forget about the court date altogether.

"They're jealous," Ellie whispered. "They just wish they could have what we have."

Jordan supposed she was right. It had been damn hard to find, and it wasn't like she hadn't tried before.

⁓

Jordan tried to convey some reassurance to Aleja, but the younger woman looked away. She couldn't blame her. She had to tell the truth, and it wasn't very helpful from where Aleja stood at the moment. Even though she was clearly not responsible for the attack on Abby, the evidence was still damning.

"Given the financial record of the defendant, we are dealing with a high flight risk. Detective Carpenter will tell us something that speaks to the danger Ms. Santos presents."

"Objection," the defense attorney intervened. "My client does not present a danger to anyone."

The judge already looked annoyed. "Counselor?"

"I apologize. We only want to establish the facts. Detective, can you describe what happened the night you first met Ms. Santos?"

Jordan straightened, feeling uncomfortable in her suit, but more so for having to tell something that would most likely influence the judge against Aleja.

"It was at the *D&T*. My...partner and I were just leaving when we witnessed an argument between two women that was getting physical."

"One of the women was Aleja Santos."

"Yes. I didn't know her name at the time. Also, no one was hurt. When they realized we were with the police, they stopped. The other woman left. Since the situation had deescalated, we left too."

"Did you file a report?" Valerie asked, unmistakable reproach in her tone. The judge looked interested and a tad impatient as Jordan took her time to answer.

"No, I didn't, and neither did Officer Harding. No one pressed charges. It was just a loud argument. Like I said, no one got hurt."

"Because you stepped in. Did you see who started it? And how physical did it get before you decided to intervene? You were off duty. I don't assume you insert yourself into every argument you witness?"

"Which question would you like me to answer first?" Jordan wished she could roll her eyes at Valerie, but of course that wasn't an option in this context.

"Do you intervene every time you witness an argument?"

"No, of course I don't."

"Detective, please tell us what happened that night."

"As I understand it, Ms. Santos was in a conversation with someone, when that woman's partner returned. They started arguing, then shouting, then pushing each other. A chair toppled over, and that's when we went over to talk to them. Things quieted down quickly. Not everyone who has a temper, will actually kill someone. I don't think Aleja Santos..."

"Thank you, Detective," Valerie said icily. "I have no more questions."

"This is not fair," Aleja shouted. "I was just talking to her, and the other girl accused me of wanting to hook up!"

"Ms. Santos," the judge warned.

"I would never harm anyone. I liked Sandra...and Mr. Ashcroft? Why would I want to kill him? He treated me better than my own parents when I first came out!"

Her lawyer hastily whispered to her and then got to his feet.

"Your Honor, I am sorry for the interruption."

"You better be."

Jordan stayed until the end, though she later wished she hadn't. Bail was set at $1 million, proof of much weight was given not only to the evidence and testimony, but the Ashcroft name. She doubted that the case of a woman found strangled in an alley would have led to the same outcome.

"Hey," Valerie called after her as she was about to leave the courthouse. "I said I'd buy you a coffee. I meant it, even though you were trying to mess with my case."

"If it's so easy to mess with it, then maybe it's on shaky ground to begin with."

Valerie laughed. "I missed you. And my case is on solid ground, believe me. How about that coffee now?"

"I don't have time. I have to get back to work." Her gaze fell on a pale looking Abigail Ashcroft and her brother Craig on the far end of the hallway. Both of them were smiling.

"Another time, then?"

"Sure," Jordan said, if only it helped her making her escape.

⚶

Whoever stabbed Abigail at the party, must have worn gloves, because her prints were the only ones on the knife. Furthermore, the caterer had confirmed that they were not missing a knife. Anyone could have had access to the regular steak knife. Jordan found Derek and Maria sitting at his desk over some papers. Jordan refrained from a comment, but she was relieved the two of them were obviously talking again. There was always a hazard when dating at work.

"Okay, the lab tells me only Abby's prints are on the knife. At the hospital, she said that she pulled out the knife herself, so that's consistent...Tell me something good," she said.

"Oh, it's good," Derek answered. "Remember those payments for Sandra Paulson, even though she wasn't employed with the firm anymore?"

"What about them?"

"We had Mrs. D'Amour look into those files, and there is someone who made payments, from another small company account that's part of the corporation. Now guess who owns this small company?"

Jordan read from the sheet he held out to her. "L. Ashcroft. Linwood? He's into pharmaceuticals and cosmetics? That's new to me, and the best thing I heard today."

"Don't get too excited. It's coincidental at this point."

"I have to agree," Maria said. "It doesn't mean he knew Sandra. It's not like he would personally write the checks."

"But he should know if payments were going through for someone not even working there? We need to ask him that. Yes, I know. Carefully," Jordan answered her partner before he could speak. "With this case, we could make a drinking game out of every time someone threatens to sue."

"I'm glad you're taking this very seriously, Detective." No one had noticed the lieutenant standing behind them. "Carpenter, Doss, you're going to follow up with Mr. Ashcroft. Henderson—my office."

Jordan suppressed a grin. She didn't envy her partner. Even with a suspect in custody, the atmosphere was still tense, especially when said suspect might be innocent after all.

Maria drove, so Jordan hung on to her own thoughts, the morning in court, the time spent with Ellie before that, and the fact that the meeting was Kathryn was still looming. Were there any results to those many tests yet, and if there were, what did that mean for either of them? Would Kathryn ask for money? If that was the case, would she be able to refuse?

"We're here," Maria announced.

Ashcroft's secretary all but jumped to her feet when she saw them coming in. "Mr. Ashcroft is in a meeting. I don't think he—"

"Don't worry, we know the way," Jordan told her. Maria followed her, obviously amused, though she didn't comment.

They walked into the room, as surprised as the two occupants: Linwood Ashcroft and his sister Abigail. For a few odd seconds, no one said anything.

"Detectives," Linwood said. "I thought we were done with visits from the police. What is it now?"

"We're really sorry to bother you again, but there are a few more questions that came up. Could we talk in private?"

He frowned. "Abby?"

"I was just about to leave anyway," his sister said as she reached for her purse. "Doctor told me to rest—I should take him at his word. Have you found the person who stabbed me yet?" She didn't wait for an answer. "I didn't think so. Have a good day anyway."

"What is this about?" Linwood asked after the heavy door fell shut. "I thought you found the killer."

"Something came up about your company Health + Life."

"Really? I own it on paper, sure, but I'm not much involved in it. As you can see, I'm very busy with my own business, and trying to keep my siblings from screwing up Dad's. What about it?"

"It's part of D'Amour Inc.?"

"That's right. Danielle and I are on the board. I met her in college, and we started this a long time ago."

"Are you aware of payments going out from Health + Life to a former D'Amour Inc. employee, Sandra Paulson?"

Someone cleared their throat behind them. "I'm sorry, Mr. Ashcroft," the secretary said. "Would you like me to bring some coffee?"

"No, thanks, we're fine. I'm sorry, Detectives, I never heard that name before. I will, however, look into it. It sounds like someone overstepped their boundaries. I'll let you know if I find anything."

"Please do that."

"If that's all, I need to get back to work. I have your number, Detective Carpenter."

"Thanks," Jordan said as she and Maria got up to leave. Ashcroft stayed behind his desk.

"First of all, was he just flirting?" Maria asked once the door was closed.

"Not a chance. He's firmly convinced I am going to hell."

"Oh, okay. Second, college? What was she, his teacher?"

"Interesting theory," Jordan said. "I'm not convinced he never knew Sandra's name. And I believe there's someone we can ask." She stepped up to the secretary's desk. The woman all but shrank back.

"Is there anything else I can help you with?" she asked hesitantly.

"Do you know this woman?" Jordan handed her the photo of Sandra Paulson.

"No."

"Are you sure?"

"I don't know what you want me to say. No, I don't know her."

"You are aware of her though?"

"I saw her name in the news, when the jogger found her. That's all."

She cast a nervous look at the door of Linwood's office.

"Thank you. If you can think of anything else, please don't hesitate to give us a call."

"Why do you think she knows something?" Maria asked later when they were on their way back to the department.

"Because she's in the best position to overhear things. She heard us mention Paulson to Linwood, and I swear she was more startled than he was. Let's drive by her apartment once more."

⁂

Half an hour later, Jordan was back at the station, standing in front of the board that detailed the facts of the murders, Gerald Ashcroft and Sandra Paulson.

Her hunches hadn't paid off as well as she'd hoped, but something different had come up. While the landlord had never seen Sandra with Linwood, she confirmed that Abigail Ashcroft had been in the apartment more than once.

Where was the connection? Sandra had been fired from D'Amour Inc. which was Abigail's competition in her latest venture, also connected to a firm owned by Linwood.

It looked like those siblings had spent a lifetime of conspiring against one another.

Given her own history, Jordan thought she had to be grateful for being an only child. Why had Abby been there if she and Linwood weren't talking? Abby didn't seem to share her younger brother's homophobic tendencies—at least—and it had been due to Craig's machinations that she was able to launch the business in the first place.

She stared at the picture of Sandra Paulson, willing the woman to give up her secrets. She was somehow the connection, Linwood, Aleja, Ashcroft senior...but she couldn't talk.

When her cell phone rang, Jordan was fairly thrilled to realize it was Linwood's secretary on the other end. Talk about hunches.

"I can't talk here. Can you meet me after my shift? I get off work at 5:30."

"Yes, of course. Is Mr. Ashcroft still in?"

"He left for a few minutes. Look, I don't even know if this is important, but I know that he signed off on the checks for Ms. Paulson. She was often in his office, sometimes more than an hour, and he would have me hold all the calls. I don't know what they were talking about, but—nothing, sir, just a wrong number." Jordan realized that Linwood must have arrived at this moment.

The call ended abruptly.

"It's not enough yet," she said to herself. "But we're getting there."

Chapter Fifteen

F or a moment, Ellie thought she had imagined Rhonda standing next to her car in the parking lot. She tugged at a strand of hair self-consciously, once more reminded of not so smart decisions, and hoped Rhonda wasn't going to insist on that coffee. She and Jordan had enough on their plate in general, and with one persistent ex in particular.

Ellie was beyond relieved that Jordan's current cases didn't require any involvement from FBI psychiatrist Dr. Bethany Roberts. Ellie had a somewhat odd relationship with her. She admired her skills. However, she got uncertain around her, and she didn't like her to be around Jordan, not more than absolutely necessary.

"Hey. Can I help you?"

"Yeah. I was going to call, but then I was pretty much just around the corner, so I decided to come by. You guys are still looking for Raphael?"

"Yes, of course. You know where he is?"

"Well, not exactly, but he asked me to meet him in a coffee shop downtown. I said yes. That's good, right? I can be there? Be the bait?"

"No, it doesn't work like that. I'll check in with Detective Rogers. He might have some questions for you. You can come with me."

Rhonda pouted. "There I thought I was getting a wire and trick him into telling me something..."

"No. Definitely no wire and tricks. Do you know if he has a gun?"

Rhonda shrugged. "Doesn't everyone?"

Yeah, that's helpful.

"Don't worry. You'll be safe."

"You know, that's kinda sexy, you taking charge like this," Rhonda said wistfully. "Sometimes I don't know why we ever broke up."

Ellie decided she didn't need to answer that.

Rogers wasn't in, but a younger detective by the name of Hargrove.

"Thank you for coming in," he told Rhonda. "We'll take it from here."

The pout was something very familiar to Ellie.

"Are you saying you don't need me for this? To distract him or something?"

Ellie winced, but Hargrove didn't seem fazed by Rhonda's disappointment.

"No, that won't be necessary. Again, thank you Ms. Marks."

"Bye," Ellie said pointedly, and Rhonda finally shrugged and walked out.

"All right, this is what we'll do. You and McCarthy will come in from the back in case he tries something. We'll bring him in, hopefully get some answers."

Ellie nodded. She knew the café, which was basically one long rectangular room, the counter stretching almost along one entire wall, the entrance in the front, a second door in the back.

The drive took less than ten minutes.

He was already sitting in the café, nervously checking his cell phone.

Ellie could tell Kate was almost as excited as Rhonda had been about the turn of events.

"Maybe this is it. Maybe we can find her today."

Yes, sometimes these cases worked out against all odds.

"Let's hope so," Ellie said as she opened the back door. Inside the café, Hargrove was talking to the woman behind the counter, then turned and walked up to the corner where the man in question was sitting.

Raphael Deane jumped to his feet and ran before he had even seen Kate and Ellie. He pushed a barista, so she stumbled and all but showered Hargrove in latte and espresso. Ellie chased after him.

"Raphael Deane? Stop! We just have a few questions for you!"

His reaction was to run faster, down the block and into an alley. Ellie was able to tackle him near inches before he would have crashed into a fence.

"I didn't do anything," he claimed. "You have no right!"

"Then why did you run?"

"That's always the way with you," Deane seethed. "You never want the truth, or explanations. You already made up your mind."

"Well, try me. Let's go downtown and have that conversation."

She wondered, however, if his cryptic words had to do with the missing woman. Ellie wanted to know, but she was also aware it wasn't her place.

Hargrove arrived shortly after.

"Whatever it is you think I've done, I'm innocent," Deane claimed.

"You're guilty of racking up my bill for the dry cleaners," Hargrove said. "For starters. Good job, Officer Harding."

"Thanks." Ellie nodded as she brushed the dirt of her uniform.

She got back to the car in time to hear the 911 call come through, from a familiar location, from a pregnant woman, alone and in distress.

Darla's baby was early.

⁓

"Could you please go? I'm tied up here. Please let me know if there's any news. I'll talk to you later."

Jordan would apologize later, as usual, she thought, tossing her phone onto the dashboard with more vehemence than necessary. She had promised Darla to be there for her, pay her back for all the times her information had helped tip a case—but when the young woman needed her the most, she was trapped waiting for Linwood's secretary. She had agreed to meet Jordan outside the building, so they could drive someplace else and talk in private. It was 5:47, and she hadn't shown up.

Jordan had tried calling her but only got the voicemail. Had she been held up upstairs? Changed her mind? Was Linwood on to her?

She went back into the building, but as she got into the elevator, a security guard stepped out.

"I'm sorry, Ma'am, you can't go up there now. There's no one there."

"Mr. Ashcroft has already left?"

"He's attending a fundraising dinner tonight."

"And his secretary?"

There was a hint of impatience in the man's expression. "Look, I told you there's no one. If you'll excuse me now. Unless you have a warrant, I need to ask you to leave."

Outside, she tried the cell phone again, and this time, the secretary picked up.

"I'm sorry, something came up," she said hastily. "I'd prefer you keep what I said between us. I might have been mistaken about Ms. Paulson."

"What? You said she spent hours in this office."

And I'm spending a lot of time waiting for you when I should be somewhere else.

"Maybe it wasn't her after all. Mr. Ashcroft sees lots of...women. I'm sorry I bothered you, Detective. Please don't come to my apartment again."

"Okay, I got it. Thank you anyway."

Jordan looked up the woman's address and requested backup before she got on her way.

Despite Rhonda's and Detective Hargrove's appreciation of her "taking charge," Ellie had listened to some stern words from Sergeant Bristol, clarifying as to who made assignments at the precinct. She knew he had a point, and he had not simply chastised her, but acknowledged that this wasn't just her doing.

Ellie knew she had to get back on track, find time to study for the detective's exam. Now that her living situation was settled for the time being, and the rest of her life was getting there, she had to make that time if she ever wanted to move forward.

It was hard to concentrate on these questions though, waiting to hear on Darla Pierson. She hoped Jordan would make it here soon—if anything happened to Darla or the baby before she arrived, Ellie knew she would be incredibly hard on herself. The perfect vacation bliss was already fading in her memory. They needed a happy ending once in a while.

She sat there for another period of time that felt like hours, when the doctor came heading her way.

"Officer, you were here for Ms. Pierson?"

"Yes. Can you tell me anything?"

"Her baby boy was born prematurely. He'll need to stay with us for a few days, but he's going to be okay."

"What about Ms. Pierson?"

"She's fine."

Ellie breathed a sigh of relief. "Can I see her?"

"Only for a short moment."

"Thank you, Doctor."

The happy ending needed a little more work, Ellie reflected as she took in Darla who looked beyond exhausted and sad.

"They wouldn't even let me hold him." Her voice was slightly slurred with the meds she'd been given. "Can you look at him for me? Please?"

"Of course. Your baby will be fine. He just needs to grow a little stronger, gain some weight."

"Maybe Jordan was right, and this was a terrible idea." There were tears in Darla's eyes. "I can't even do this right. What kind of mother—"

"You're going to be great once you've had some time to recover. Meanwhile, they're going to take good care of him here."

"Where's Jordan?" Darla asked.

Ellie would have liked to know herself. "She couldn't leave work. She'll be here as soon as she can. Someone's going to chase me out sometime soon, but I'll stay in the waiting room."

"Thank you." Darla gave her a weak smile.

"It's no problem. Get some rest, okay?"

"I agree with that," the nurse said behind her. "Officer?"

"Sure. I'm coming."

Keeping her promise, she got to take a look at the tiny baby in the incubator. As she stood in front of the window, Ellie had an idea. She quickly took a picture on her cell phone and snuck back into Darla's room for a moment so she could show her. After asking Darla's permission, she sent it to Jordan as well in case she couldn't make it tonight.

The sight stayed with her, giving her a lot to think about. Ellie couldn't imagine having a baby at Darla's age. She could hardly imagine it now, though Jordan's adoptive mother seemed to harbor some hope that motherhood was in the near future for them. Jordan was reluctant though not completely opposed. At some point, Ellie would have to make up her mind on how she felt about the subject.

Still no sign of Jordan. She wondered if Kathryn was still here, but decided this time, not to let curiosity get the better of her.

⁂

Derek met her at the secretary's apartment, and together, they approached the front door. It swung open when Jordan pushed lightly, giving sight to the mess inside, broken glass, a chair toppled over. A quick search revealed that there was no one in the apartment.

"He lied to us about Paulson, and now his secretary is missing after she wanted to talk to us about this exact subject. That's enough to crash the party," Jordan said.

Derek looked dubious. "I'm not sure your friend Esposito will agree."

"There are so many things wrong with this sentence. Come on, let's get a unit in here. I think you and I have a fundraising event to attend."

"Sounds like fun," he said.

"Yeah. And he might know about this too." She held up a piece of wire in a gloved hand. "Someone has a real penchant for using these."

"Can I see your invitations, please?" the young blonde woman asked in a pleasant tone, regardless of the fact that they weren't dressed for the occasion. Well, Derek might have passed, and her eyes were mainly on him anyway.

"There you go," Jordan said, placing her badge in front of her. The woman's eyes went wide.

"We need to speak to Mr. Ashcroft."

She had heard before about the group hosting the event, and it was enough for her not to have much patience with any woman who associated herself with this. This was a group of old boys who wanted to restore society to the "good old times"—good for no one but them.

"I don't know..."

"It's urgent. Thank you."

"Um...okay then. He's at table #14." She returned Derek's smile with an uncertain one of her own.

"Thanks so much, Cordelia. Wouldn't hurt you to be a little more polite," he told Jordan as they walked past the entrance.

"Did you see what this event is all about? I'm not going to shake anyone. That's about as polite as I can get. This is the opposite of what Ashcroft worked for."

"Well, we know Linwood hangs with a different crowd. And here we are. Mr. Ashcroft, we have to ask you to come with us."

"Is this a joke?" Ashcroft's wife asked. "You have more questions that need answers now? This is important."

"A life might be at stake. I believe you would agree that's more important. Mr. Ashcroft?"

Realizing that conversation at other tables had stopped, he put a smile on this face before he got to his feet, his tone a clear contradiction to what he wanted to convey to his peers.

"You've gone too far, Detective. I wonder if your workplace has a non-discrimination clause for people like you. I'd be surprised."

"Yeah, we can discuss all that later," Jordan said, unimpressed with his antics. The lieutenant had long been aware of her relationship with Bethany that neither of them had cared to hide. Firing her for being gay would be the last thing on his mind.

Chapter Sixteen

Jordan hadn't forgotten the warnings about how to deal with the Ashcroft family, but a life was at stake. Now that she finally had Linwood Ashcroft in an interrogation room, she'd make the most of it.

"Ms. Ryan wanted to discuss your relationship with Ms. Paulson. When I went to pick her up, she was gone. The guard told me she'd left, later we had another phone call where she directed us to her apartment which has been wrecked. Where is she, Linwood?"

"You guys are hilarious," he said. "All of this...my lawyer here will have a field day in court, and you, Detective, can say goodbye to your badge."

"Linwood," his attorney, a mild-mannered man in his late fifties, said. "We'll cross that bridge if we get to it. I don't believe the detective has an agenda. She's just doing her job, right?"

Jordan decided it sounded too condescending to merit an answer, instead she continued.

"Why did you lie to us about Sandra? You knew her. You signed off on paychecks for her, from a firm she was no longer working for—why is that?"

"I don't know what Ms. Ryan told you, but it sounds like she made a lot of stuff up. I was going to let her go soon, maybe she found out. In any case, I'm shocked you're taking her word over—"

"There are security tapes that show you and Ms. Paulson. In your firm, and the hotel across the street. Did your wife know about these meetings?"

"You're bluffing. What, you want to blackmail me with this story?"

"Wait a second," the lawyer now intervened. "Where are those tapes?"

"What are you getting out of it?" Linwood questioned.

"What I want to get out of it is to not find another body. We are still going over the tapes. Be assured we'll inform you if anything else important comes up. Mr. Ashcroft, if you tell us where Ms. Ryan is, we can still do something for you."

"How about you let me go, and we forget about this ridiculous idea? She was never that reliable. Maybe she just took off."

"And you still employed her for over ten years? That's curious," Derek said from where he was leaning against the wall. "What exactly was the nature of your relationship with Sandra Paulson? Why the money?" He shrugged. "You accused Detective Carpenter of bluffing and wanting to blackmail you at the same time. There wouldn't be much to blackmail you with if it was all a bluff. We can show you those tapes if you want, by the way."

"All right, I admit it! Sandra was in a tight spot after Danielle fired her. I wanted to get rid of Health + Life, and I'd been talking to Danielle about it. That's where I met Sandra, she came to interview here, but things turned out differently, and...I was just helping her out."

"So she owed you."

"If you want to call it that."

"Did she help you frame Aleja Santos? You had to get rid of the witness, that's it?"

"Detectives, why don't you take a break?"

All eyes went to the lieutenant standing in the doorway.

"I guess your supervisor doesn't like what you're insinuating either," Linwood said. "I'm glad someone's finally showing common sense."

"Mr. Ashcroft. I had a call from Congressman Bond."

"Is that so? What did he say?"

Jordan remembered the man from Abby's party, angrily demanding they'd let everyone go.

"I assume you already know. I told him I had no intention bringing that kind of politics into the workplace. My detectives picked you up for a reason. Their private matters are of no relevance here."

Jordan was aware of Derek's questioning look, and she shrugged. The bluff went both ways, apparently. They had the tapes, but their colleagues were still working on finding anything damning on them. Ashcroft had quickly made good on his threat and was trying to throw his power around.

"Is it not? Aleja Santos is homosexual also. Detective Carpenter testified that she met her in a bar, and isn't it interesting that she's hell-bent on clearing her? You don't think that's a conflict of interest?"

"Sounds like it, but I think you should stop talking now. Linwood, come on, you know better than that," his lawyer chastised. "I'd like to confer with my client in private, please."

Jordan shook her head and got up to leave the room. Derek and the lieutenant followed her outside.

"He planned the whole thing. He had access to the meds, he knew Sandra. Maybe she did it freely, maybe he used her situation to send her after Aleja. He must have somehow caught Ms. Ryan when she talked to me." She didn't like the lieutenant's concerned expression. "You don't think I'd coddle a suspect because she's a lesbian?"

He sighed. "No, Carpenter, I don't think that, but I could do without calls from congressmen lecturing me on my hiring practices. Wrap this up and do it quickly. Find Ryan."

"...but tread carefully?"

"Don't push it," he warned. "You won't be able to talk to Ashcroft again before tomorrow. So until then, it would be great if you could come up with something."

"I'll check in with the night shift, make sure they're on the lookout for Ryan," Jordan said. "There's somewhere I need to go after."

"I can pass it on to the night shift," Derek offered. "I'll meet you back here later."

"Thank you. I won't be long."

Ellie had left a message to tell her that Darla and her newborn baby would be okay, picture included, but she still felt the urgency when she finally got in the car to get to the hospital. She was tired, and had a long night ahead of her. Probably they wouldn't even let her see Darla or the baby, but she had made a promise.

Ellie couldn't believe what Jordan just told her.

"Really, he can do that, call on his congressman buddy for this BS? Doesn't the guy have a job to do?" They were still in the hospital, and even if they hadn't been, she didn't have the energy to raise her voice. Jordan didn't seem much concerned about the situation, not enough in Ellie's opinion. "God, where does it stop?"

"Relax. They're not going to do anything. Once we find Ryan, it's all over, and I don't think the congressman wants to be seen as too chummy with a murderer."

"Yeah, until the next time someone wants to throw their weight around."

"The lieutenant understands the situation. No one is going to get fired just because we had a few drinks at *D&T*."

"I know. I'm sorry. I guess I really need to go home." Seeing Jordan's longing gaze, she almost wished she hadn't said that. "You can come join me whenever you get out today. Good luck with Ryan."

"Thanks. Anything new on the missing girl?"

"Deane is still in custody, that's all I know."

"Okay. Good night, and thanks for waiting. I'll see you later. I hope."

"Yeah, me too."

They shared a quick kiss before Jordan went to check on Darla, and Ellie headed for her car.

When Ellie entered the apartment, it was one of the rare occasions when she was alone. She had gotten used to having another roommate quickly, especially since she and Kate had been friends for a few years now. Jordan, while she insisted she wanted to keep the house "in the woods," as Ellie called it, was around often, and so was Derek Henderson.

Tonight, it was eerily quiet. She had planned to take a long hot bath and relax with a book, but the evening turned out not to be much relaxing after all. Her thoughts were drawn back to Darla and her challenging situation. What revelations would Kathryn have for Jordan this weekend?

Then, there were the regular threats of lawsuits from the Ashcroft family, which Linwood had taken to a new level. Growing up in a more liberal environment, Ellie hadn't been confronted with odds like this before, men like Linwood and the congressman throwing their weight around for some sort of sick power play. She had always thought it was enough to go after the bad guys, but some of them did a lot of damage without ever breaking a law.

She didn't take Jordan's reassurances lightly. If she could have a career in this department, so could Ellie, but it could involve an uphill battle she hadn't faced much before.

There was a sound, like someone dropping something on the floor, startling her out of her thoughts.

"Kate?"

Silence. She got out of the bath and wrapped a towel around herself, feeling trapped with the bathroom door closed. Ellie carefully turned the knob, aware that her hand was trembling. Even now, it wasn't completely clear how Ward had made it into her place at the time. Danny Roth apparently didn't know, and she had no memory of what happened that night. The living/dining area and the kitchen looked like she'd left it before, the front door still closed. Her heart was hammering. It took her only a few seconds to determine that both her own and Kate's rooms were undisturbed. The sound had to have come from the hallway. Still clad in the towel, she took a deep breath, leaning against the locked front door.

Everything was fine.

It would get better with time.

Ellie poured herself a glass from the open bottle of white wine in the fridge, willing herself to calm down. Moving on, eyes on the prize...She just wished she wasn't alone any longer in the usually lively apartment.

Cursing Roth and his fantasy of playing hero opposite of a crook like Ward, she lay in bed not much later, feeling exhausted. Sleep came with visions of darkness, the rectangle of a covered-up window and the feel of the cuff around her wrist.

"Hey. Ellie, you're okay. It was just a dream."

Jordan's soft whisper was fortunately reality. Ellie snuggled into her arms with a sigh.

"Sorry. You can't have gotten much sleep. Did you find the secretary?"

"No," Jordan said, sounding frustrated. "I missed her by maybe five minutes, and she dropped off the face of the earth? I'll have the warrant by tomorrow. Linwood had plenty of time to do whatever he did to her before he went to the dinner, and I'm going to prove it. This family is too much. He hopes to get me fired because I'm a lesbian, and his brother thinks we're family."

"Yeah. They all have something to hide. It's a shame that with the dad they had, they still turned out this way. There's not much online about the mother, but she seemed like a nice woman too, worked in the business and with the charities."

Jordan was silent at that, perhaps thinking of the strange ways biology and upbringing interacted. It was one thing to push her to communicate with Kathryn, because of Ellie's own regrets and omissions. When she thought of a twelve-year-old taken out of a family because no one seemed to give a damn, it reminded her Jordan had reason to be very cautious where her biological parents were concerned.

"When can we go on vacation again?" she asked.

Jordan laughed. "Not anytime soon, I'm afraid, but once this mess is sorted out, we could have a nice dinner somewhere out of town, maybe stay at a hotel for one night, just to get away from everything."

"I'd love that."

This time, the silence didn't bother Ellie, and she drifted off into a more restful sleep.

Chapter
Seventeen

"You took all the hot water again," Jordan accused her partner who was sitting at the dining table with a coffee. "So it's only fair you talk to the lieutenant first. He's not going to be happy."

"Maybe someone needed a cold shower more."

"Maybe someone is talking about things that are none of his business."

She caught Ellie and Kate sharing an amused look at the banter. "All right. We're going to need more to keep Linwood in custody. Ms. Ryan seemed pretty savvy. Maybe there is something on the computer, in her office."

"Did you find anything on the tapes?" Ellie asked.

"Linwood and Sandra, yes. That puts him with Sandra, though not necessarily on the night she died. He has means and motive, for the murders and framing Aleja, but if that's all, he'll make bail this morning." Jordan put her mug down. "Come on. We have to go and ask Bristol for some of the kids."

"You know you can't call us that anymore, right?" Kate said. "Because it's really awkward."

"Right," Ellie chimed in. "Remember who's paying for all that hot water you're bickering about."

"Okay, I'll give you that. We're all done here?"

"Ready," Ellie said quietly, aware of Jordan's impatient tone. Time was running out in many ways. It was impossible to forget that they'd both been on the other side of that equation.

Later, when requesting officers to serve the warrant, Jordan thought she must have imagined the flash of annoyance on Sergeant Bristol's face. Sure, McCarthy had spent a lot of time working with Rogers. It wasn't her fault when her case overlapped with Ellie's duties, was it?

"Remember, we're looking for any hint as to where he might have taken her, and a possible connection—or lack thereof—to Aleja Santos. Officer Marshall, I'd like you to assist Officer Atwood with the hotline, any hint to her whereabouts goes straight to me or Detective Henderson." Libby nodded, though her expression was terse, making Jordan wonder whether she was aware of the gossip Atwood had been spinning.

"Good. I'll see you there. Thanks, Sergeant."

"You're welcome, Detective."

It was with some satisfaction that Jordan realized the same security guard was on duty this morning.

"Mr. Ellis. You said to come back with a warrant. Here we are."

He snorted but made no move to stop them. "I don't know what you're expecting to find," he said. "I told you yesterday, the secretary left at 5:30, Mr. Ashcroft, a few minutes later."

That probably meant she had never left the building.

With the search underway, Jordan checked in with Libby once more to learn that there was no substantial hit from the hotline. She called Valerie who picked up right away.

"When are you going to give me a suspect who actually looks good? I'm already in hot water regarding Santos, and that's before Ashcroft's hearing."

"Ashcroft is going down, sooner or later. When we find Ryan..."

"If you find her, alive, that is. Good luck, Jordan. Keep me posted, okay?"

"Will do. Wait, sorry, there's another call."

"Well, yeah, I know it's been a long time."

"Funny. I've got to take this. See you."

The other caller was Abigail Ashcroft, and Jordan braced herself for more or less righteous indignation.

"Detective, it's you, thank God."

The whisper on the other end of the line didn't sound like she was going to chastise Jordan for anything, much less threaten with a lawsuit. She had read all the testimonies, interviewed some of the guests. No one had seen anything. Mrs. Santos had no idea who could have manipulated the breakers, and she had been in the kitchen the whole time.

"Mrs. Ashcroft, how can I help you?"

"I was wondering if you could come see me."

"I'm busy right now. Would it be okay if I—?"

"Detective, I'm scared. I think I'm remembering something...I don't want to talk on the phone. Could you come to my house?"

Jordan cast a look across the room where officers were still busy searching the office. Nothing had turned up so far. This was a recipe for disaster. They needed something on Ashcroft, or he would go free.

"I'll be there in a few minutes. Don't let anyone in, okay? Your daughter's still in school?"

"She's on a field trip out of town today. Detective Carpenter, I heard you arrested Linwood." She didn't wait for an answer, but said, "That's probably a good idea."

Jordan went to inform Derek that she was going to see Abby. "I'm going to need some backup," she said.

Derek nodded. "We're almost done here. I'll send Lyons and McCarthy, and I'll check in with Esposito after."

"Thanks. If Ashcroft gets off, we need to put a tail on him. If Ryan is still alive, that's where he's going to go."

"I agree. See you later."

"Yeah. Let's hope Abby has something for us after all."

It would be a good day, Jordan reflected, if they could finally wrap up the case and she could see Darla tonight. At this rate, the younger woman was probably thinking she was avoiding her. Jordan admitted to herself that she still felt guilty about her initial reaction to Darla's pregnancy, all mixed up with her own issues about motherhood, something she would have to get over eventually. She had to squeeze in a visit somehow.

In the parking lot of the Ashcroft house, she saw Abigail's car and a new truck. Did it belong to her—or was someone else with her?

Abby opened the door wide, nervously smoking a cigarette.

"Come on in, Detective. I'm glad you came."

"Is there anyone in the house with you?"

"No. I just wanted to talk to you. What's with the cavalry? You're not planning on arresting me too?"

"Ms. Ashcroft. You asked me to come."

"Yeah. Can they wait outside? It's kind of private."

Jordan made a sign to the officers in the squad car, Kate McCarthy and Casey Lyons. "I can't stay long. As you know, we're in the middle of an investigation."

"Just humor me for a moment, will you?"

Her behavior was odd, too odd for Jordan to send the officers away yet.

"They'll wait outside. Okay. What is it you wanted to tell me?"

Abby led her into the living room where she had prepared tea and a plate with cookies for two. Jordan's stomach growled at the sight. Her fault that she had cut breakfast short—however, there was no time for the indulgences offered by her host.

"Abby."

"Yes, I'll get to it. Will you sit down?"

Jordan perched on the edge of one of the armchairs.

"Why did you think arresting Linwood was a good idea? If you know anything, Abby, now would be a good time to tell us. We know he sent regular checks to a woman he admitted was his mistress. This woman is dead now."

"You think he killed Dad?" Abby asked, her eyes wide. She nearly burned her fingers on the cigarette butt and immediately lit another. "I'm sorry, I smoke too much when I'm nervous, especially when my daughter is not in the house, and I have no reason...I need to know how much you have on Linwood. Forget what I said earlier. I heard Santos might be released from prison soon, and I'm afraid she might go after me next."

"With all due respect, that doesn't make sense. She was already in custody when you held your launch party."

"Yes, but Mrs. Santos wasn't. They hate all of us. Well, Linwood has done a lot of things to make people hate him, but she and her niece had it in for all of us."

"You're saying Mrs. Santos stabbed you?"

"Yes. I remember now. It was her."

"You must be mistaken. People saw her in the kitchen the whole time."

Abby scoffed. "And you believe them? Of course they covered for her. They don't want to lose their jobs."

"Well, it's you and your brothers now who have the authority, not your father or Mrs. Santos. You are certain you saw her?"

"Why would I say it if I didn't mean it? They want to frame one of us for it, first it was Craig because of the money, now Linwood. If the charges don't stick, I'll be next."

Jordan was beginning to ask herself if Abigail was paranoid, or just that good an actress.

"Your father and Mrs. Santos were in love. I think all of you had trouble accepting it."

"Oh, please, Detective, don't turn this around on me. You don't kill the people you love."

"Can I ask you a question? Who does the truck in the parking lot belong to?"

"Why do you want to know?"

"Just curious."

"It's mine."

Jordan could see the alarm on Abby's face when her brother Craig walked in, answering her question.

"Why is it important?" he asked. "Abby is telling you what she saw. You don't believe her?"

"Craig, did you lend the car to anyone recently?"

Abby looked upset, but she didn't say anything. Her eyes held a clear warning.

"I don't have to answer these questions. Why don't you go arrest Mrs. Santos? Abby identified her as her attacker."

"I assume you don't consider Aleja Santos 'family' in this context," Jordan said. "You have been very helpful to your sister lately, helping out with money and all. Linwood...I'm not so sure. He had his own little scheme going with Sandra and Health + Life. Did you know that we've been looking for a vehicle exactly like this? There were tracks from a truck like that at the scene where we found Sandra Paulson. I'd be surprised if the pattern didn't match."

"Why don't we all calm down for a moment and stop accusing each other?" Abigail suggested. "I know what I saw. Mrs. Santos could have easily given Dad those pills, he trusted her. And Aleja was involved with Sandra Paulson somehow. If she killed her, of course they helped each other out. Detective, you seem hungry. Why don't you have a tea and a cookie before you go over to Dad's house? Or better even, send away those officers outside. They are making me nervous."

"That's a good idea," Craig agreed, picking a cookie from the plate. "Let's not make accusations no one can prove. Everything is fine, Detective Carpenter. This tells me though that you're grasping at straws. This truck is hardly a unique model."

"I have another question," Jordan said. "Why was Ms. D'Amour uninvited from the launch party? Did you just find out about Linwood paying Sandra from one of the Health + Life accounts? Is that why you went to see him?"

The siblings exchanged another look.

"Craig, Aleja told me she trusted you. You were the first she came out to, and I believe that just like your father, you were always decent to her. Why would you want her to be convicted of a crime she didn't commit?"

Craig looked uncertain for a moment. "There's not enough evidence against her either. I don't know what you're talking about."

"Then who is it you are protecting?"

"My father's legacy," Linwood Ashcroft said as he joined them. "The image of my father from when he was still sane. You're surprised, Detective? I told you I have friends in high places. I've done a lot of favors over the years, that's how it works—it was rather easy to collect. There's not going to be a trial. Now, you should leave. We have things to talk about."

"Did you drive the truck the night Sandra Paulson died?"

Jordan saw Abby twisting a strand of hair between her thumb and forefinger nervously, and she remembered the two of them sitting in Linwood's office.

"Linwood is right. You should leave."

This would probably be her last chance. "All right. You had an opportunity to tell the truth. I'll have to get back now and see Ms. Ryan." They were on edge, all of them, but this little bluff would hopefully keep them from doing something stupid. "I believe she'll have some interesting things to tell us when she wakes up. Have a good day." Jordan got up and walked to the front door, a shiver of foreboding tingling down her spine before Linwood said, "Don't move. Put your hands up."

Jordan obliged, slowly turning around. So much for the effect of that bluff.

"That's a bad idea," she said. "I have a unit waiting for me outside. They're going to figure out something's not right pretty soon. Abby, Craig, whatever you knew before, you don't want to be involved in this."

"Shut up," Linwood said. "Sit. You're going to call them off right now. You want a story? I'll give you one."

"Linwood," Craig warned. "Now's not the time."

"That's right," Abigail said, getting to her feet. "Hard as it is to imagine, I have a business to run. Thanks, Dad, but no thanks."

"You want to go now?" Linwood spoke, but both men looked at their sister in disbelief. "Don't you think we have something more important to take care of?"

She gave a bored shrug. "You created this mess. Fix it."

"I can't believe this." Craig shook his head.

The pieces came together rapidly—it all fit. Still, Jordan was stunned as to what the conclusion appeared to be. Linwood was without a doubt guilty, but he wasn't the only one. Plus, whatever arrangement they had made together, it obviously stood on shaky ground.

"Just one thing—did you all hate your father so much, or was it all about getting back at Mrs. Santos? Sandra Paulson, I assume, was just collateral damage. You really thought this was going to work out even though you were already stabbing each other in the back five minutes later? No offense, Abby."

Linwood's finger tightened on the trigger of the gun he was holding. "Make that call now."

"All right, relax. I'm calling, okay?"

"No tricks."

"I got you. Hey, Casey. I'm about to wrap things up in here. Why don't you go back and tell Derek he can get started with Ms. Ryan."

"I thought you hadn't found her yet." Casey sounded surprised, which was a good start. "Did you hear that Mr. Ashcroft got out? Esposito is livid. Maybe you should come back here yourself..."

"I will soon. Make sure Derek asks her about—"

"That's enough." Linwood took the phone out of her hand and turned it off.

"That's not going to help."

"I agree with her," Craig said sarcastically. "Great job, Linwood, you think that's going to make them go away? You're just like Abby, thinking it's a great idea to stab yourself. I'm surrounded by morons."

"Shut up," Abby seethed at him. "If it weren't for your money problems, no one would have even suspected any of us."

Jordan saw that Linwood's attention was on his siblings, and she slowly moved her hand towards her gun. Then the doorbell rang, and for a moment, everyone seemed frozen.

"I'll go," Abby said. "I don't think they'll trust either of you at this point. Talk about morons."

Linwood was back waving the revolver in her face. "Be quiet, or I swear you'll regret it."

Chapter Eighteen

Both Kate and Casey had a bad feeling even before the call was dropped. Ryan hadn't been found yet, and someone had interrupted Jordan. Kate, too, noticed the truck in its parking spot and the wide tires as they walked up the steps to Abigail Ashcroft's house. Casey rang the doorbell, and a few moments later, the owner appeared.

"Ms. Ashcroft, it is important that we talk to Detective Carpenter."

"I'll tell her," Abigail said, sounding eerily cheerfully. "Don't worry, she's fine, but for some reason the cell phone reception can be horrible in here. Considering what I pay for it, I really should change the provider."

"Ms. Ashcroft..."

"I'll send her right out. Thank you, officers."

The door was closed nearly in their faces.

"I'd like to run the license plate on that truck while we wait," Kate said. "I have a feeling the owner could be inside."

"Let's call it in," Casey agreed.

⟡

"This isn't going to work. They'll be back."

"Well, meanwhile you will have left for a place unknown. I was never here, and Craig and Abby, they have no idea. That can totally work because for the most part, it's true."

"So charming," Abby remarked. "It's no wonder Sandra was going to bail on you. If you weren't giving them money or tying them up, no one would ever want to be around you. What are we going to do with her now?"

"She's right, they'll be back, and this time, they'll come in if they think something's wrong. I say we don't wait too long," Craig said.

"Ugh. Don't get blood on these new carpets." Abby went to the window, peering outside from behind the curtains. "What are they still doing here? Oh, I guess they're leaving now, good. I want this to be over before Savannah comes back."

Jordan wondered how she could be so dissociated from the situation that she had no trouble talking about her daughter, and blood on the carpet, in one breath. She couldn't believe these grown people bickering like twelve-year-olds while casually discussing the murder of two people. She was alarmed but not scared. Kate and Casey would have gotten the message, and the place would be swarming with cops soon.

"Abby, if you don't put a stop to this, there's a good chance you'll never see your daughter again."

"Don't believe her," Craig said. "They have nothing on you."

"Abby. You sacrificed a lot already. Craig has money invested in your firm. Linwood was in bed with your competition. You think they care?"

Abby came closer, studying Jordan curiously. "You still don't get it, do you? When your colleagues come looking for you, I'll tell them the same thing I told you earlier. I saw Mrs. Santos. Maybe she went after you too because she knew she was going to prison. What happened at the party, I did that. And it worked. I am off the hook, Linwood and Craig have alibis, but Mrs.

Santos only has the word of the hired staff in the kitchen. I have a knife here, with her prints on it. Convenient, isn't it?"

"So, you all have each other's back, is that right? Craig, it doesn't bother you at all that your brother raises money for people who associate with the 'gays are an abomination' crowd?"

If only to make the situation more absurd, both men looked at each other and laughed. Abigail looked amused.

"All right, clean up this mess now, will you? I'll talk to you later."

She left through the back door, and moments later, Jordan heard the sound of an engine running. Good. They might be cocky, but they weren't very clever. The police would pick up Abigail, which left Linwood and Craig. The latter shook his head.

"Detective, you wouldn't understand. When you get to where we are, these little differences don't matter. I certainly don't care about getting married. Looking at my siblings' marriages, that's not exactly something to strive for. Small minds are easy to manipulate. If you tell them the right lines, they give you money—they same goes for my sister-in-law's family."

Appealing to his conscience was clearly not the right angle. "You might not care about 'family' all that much, that's all right. With the murder of a cop, not even your small-minded friends will be able to bail you out."

"I guess we'll have to take that chance," Craig said. "Why don't we take this party downstairs? Let's not ruin Abby's precious carpets."

It occurred to Jordan that he might have been the one to drive the truck that night and maybe taking out Sandra Paulson hadn't been Linwood's idea after all.

Casey, Kate, any minute now would be fine.

They had confirmation that the truck parked in the front was registered to Craig Ashcroft. A moment later, the garage door opened to reveal Abigail Ashcroft, speeding away in her car.

"This is weird," Casey remarked. "I can stay here. You go after her, and I'll call for backup."

Kate didn't waste any time getting back into the car. Trying his cell phone, she got hold of Derek right away.

"Hey. We're still at Abigail Ashcroft's house. She just left, but Jordan is inside."

"What do you mean?"

"Her call was interrupted. Abigail came to the door, said it was the cell phone reception, but there's a truck sitting in the parking spot that belongs to Craig Ashcroft. Casey is now waiting there for backup. Where are you?"

"I just left Linwood's office. I'm still in the financial district."

"Perfect. Abigail is going South on Lincoln. She's driving a silver BMW. We need to talk to her."

"I agree. Stay behind her. I'm not far. If you stop her first, be careful."

Kate thought that assessment was optimistic, but she confirmed anyway. "Will do. On the corner of Lincoln and Pine now."

"I'll be right there."

She listened to him request another unit and heard Ellie answer. Meanwhile, Abigail was driving to the harbor where lots of office buildings were located.

What was happening inside the house?

❧

After getting back into her car, Ellie had caught the last sentences from dispatch: Abigail Ashcroft was wanted for questioning in the cases of her father and Sandra Paulson. Ellie couldn't help feeling like she'd missed something important, but she was close to the location where Abigail's vehicle was last seen, so she answered the call. She heard another siren not far away but got a visual moments later when she rounded the block that led down to the harbor. Ashcroft made no move to slow down, obviously hoping her flashy little sports car could outrun Ellie's vehicle. Ellie had no intention of letting her do that.

At the precinct, techs were still going through Ryan's computer, though as far as she knew, they hadn't found anything as to her whereabouts yet.

Ashcroft's car came to a screeching halt near an old warehouse, blocked by another car that had appeared out of nowhere. Ellie got out and saw Derek leave the other vehicle, hand on his gun. Kate arrived a minute later.

"Ms. Ashcroft, step out of the car right now, with your hands where I can see them!"

Ellie approached cautiously from the back. After a few tense moments, the door opened, and Abigail emerged from the vehicle, hands in the air.

"Don't shoot me, I didn't do anything! It's my brother Craig. He's nuts. Your colleague is in there with him right now. I barely made it out. I thought he was going to kill all of us."

She broke down crying in the middle of the street, and Derek put the cuffs on her.

Ellie stood, frozen in shock at the implications of what she'd just heard.

"We have to go."

Henderson didn't argue. "We'll take her to the house with us, and she's going to tell us exactly what is going on in there."

"I'll take her," Kate said. "Are you okay to drive?" she asked Ellie.

"Yes, of course. Let's go." Both of them went to their respective squad car and followed Derek back to Abigail's house.

When Derek Henderson called his partner, he didn't expect her to pick up so quickly after Kate and Lyons' report.

"Where are you?"

"I'm on my way. Wait for me?"

That wasn't true. He knew Jordan's car still sat in its spot in front of Ashcroft's house. He was looking at it right now.

"We're coming in."

"No, it's all right. I'll be with you in—"

"Jordan?"

"I'm holding a gun to your partner's head right now, and I might be a bit nervous. If you try to come in, I can't guarantee anything."

"No one needs to get hurt," Derek said, wishing Ellie wasn't close, listening intently. "Let's talk. Tell me what you want."

"You could show some good will and get out of here right now. You have five minutes. I see any cops out there, this will go badly," Linwood said.

"The place is surrounded. Turn yourself in. Abby already did. It's the only way for you to—"

"No! No, it's not the only way. You want her alive, don't you?"

"Yes, Linwood, of course."

"Then make sure those cops go away, and I might let her go once I'm safe."

"Might is not good enough."

"Pity, that all you'll get." He disconnected the call.

"She's doing okay," he said, if only for his and Ellie's comfort. "Him, not so much."

"Craig Ashcroft might still be in there. The truck is his. We have to move soon."

"If you come in through the front door, he'll see you coming," Abby supplied. "He killed that poor girl Sandra. He won't hesitate."

"Then we won't come through the front," Derek said grimly.

"You stupid idiot, what have you done?" Craig yelled. "Now what? They're going to storm the freaking house in a few minutes!"

"That's all right. We won't be here. We'll get down to the garage and go on a little ride with the detective. They won't do anything as long as she's with us."

"You think so? They'll have sharpshooters waiting for us outside."

"Then we need to be careful not to give them a clear shot," Linwood dismissed his concerns. "This was bound to happen at some point. We're prepared."

Jordan didn't think they were prepared at all, acting all over the place which could be to her advantage. She doubted either of them had ever dealt with a situation like this.

"Look, Craig is right. If you turn yourself in now, no one's going to get shot."

Neither man listened to her. "Get the car ready," Linwood said. "We'll be right there."

Craig stalked out of the room in angry strides.

"You're really prepared to go out there? Let me take care of this. If I talk to them..."

"Walk!"

He pushed her forward along the hallway. Bracing herself, Jordan winced at the pull on the stitches. She couldn't focus on that now. Linwood was obviously not to be reasoned with, but at the moment, they were alone in the hallway, and he lowered the gun for a moment to open the door. She kicked the gun out of his hand, and it skittered across the floor. Linwood cursed, diving for it, but she was faster.

"Not this direction," she said, catching her breath. "We're going right out front, and you'll open that garage door."

There were rapid footsteps on the stairs, and a moment later, Derek appeared on the other side of the hallway.

"Get down, Mr. Ashcroft." She picked up her cuffs and fastened them around his wrists, for a split-second distracted by the stain of red on the bandage.

"Hey," she said to Derek, "It's about time. It's a good moment though. I'm glad you're here to witness it. Mr. Ashcroft, you're under arrest for the murder of Gerald Ashcroft and Sandra Paulson."

"It wasn't me! Craig and Abby did everything!"

"Save it for the judge."

At this point, Jordan was not only disgusted, but she felt slightly dizzy.

"What about the other two?" she asked.

"We got Craig the moment he came out of the garage, trying to make his getaway. Ellie picked up Abigail, who swears it was all her brothers."

"Nice bunch," she said. "Let's get out of here. You got anything on Ryan?"

"Not yet. I assume Mr. Ashcroft will tell us right now."

"I don't know where she is. I was at the fundraiser that night, remember?"

Ellie came rushing in. "Are you okay?" Regardless of the audience, she gave Jordan a quick hug.

"Peachy. Careful," she said with regard to the blood staining the bandage.

Linwood Ashcroft regarded the scene with revulsion.

"You *are* going to hell," he predicted.

Even though it was hard to ignore the pain now, Jordan had to laugh at the absurdity.

"Wherever I go from here, I'm pretty sure it's better than where you are going. The whole act with the stairs was pretty evil to begin with, but throwing in those meds to make sure the job would be finished? Your own father. Wow."

"He wasn't supposed to die," Linwood mutter.

"I can't wait for you to tell me all about it."

"Yeah, right after you have a doctor look at this," Derek commented. "Don't worry about missing anything. They will all be with us for a while."

"I'll drive you," Ellie said, and between the two of them, Jordan didn't feel like they were giving her much room to argue.

❧

With a fresh bandage, after having a quick, strong coffee, she sat across from Linwood Ashcroft about an hour later. Ashcroft's lawyer was a lot more humble than the last time she'd seen him, and announced that his client was ready to make a full confession.

"You said you didn't mean for your father to die. What was the plan?"

"Craig and Abby, they got careless and greedy, okay? They wanted everything, and what are they going to do with it? Craig's going to burn it all with poker and on the racetrack, Abby will find a new business to work into the ground like all the others before."

"So, you're the good son?"

"I never took money from my father that I wasn't entitled to, and I always paid my loans back. You looked at my firm—it was thriving. I deserved more recognition than that, but I assume Dad had some sort of addictive nature as well."

"How so?"

"All this charity crap? Give a few thousand bucks for starving children in Africa if you must, but you don't turn your back on your own flesh and blood! He was just throwing money at those activists, helping them with their agenda."

Jordan cast a look at Derek whose expression was somewhere between amused, baffled, and put off. She felt the same. She had seen greed before, but the entitlement the Ashcroft siblings were feeling was on a whole different level.

"Killing your own flesh and blood? That's kind of harsh."

"I told you, he wasn't supposed to die. Those meds should have just slowed him down for a bit. If I had power of attorney, I would have seen to it that the reckless spending ended."

"What you call reckless spending," Derek said, "benefited hundreds, if not thousands of underprivileged kids, helped others get therapy rather than put them into prison. You didn't think that was a good thing?"

"Why is it my problem if other people make bad choices?"

"You're right," Jordan said. "Your problems right now are your own bad choices. So why frame Aleja and her aunt?"

"Are you kidding me? Santos was taking advantage of my father. She was going through his money faster than those charities did. The niece, she walked right into it. It was too easy."

"But then, there was the problem with Sandra. That was your plan too, wasn't it, for her to be seen with Aleja, right?"

"I paid her the money, but everything regarding Sandra was Craig's idea. You'll have to ask him."

"Don't worry, we will. It just surprises me that you let him have that much control, that you didn't care about what happened to your mistress."

He shrugged. "After she slept with Aleja, I didn't have any use for her anymore. She wanted to go to the police. After everything had worked out, we couldn't let that happen."

"I guess not. You're telling me that you have no idea what happened to her other than you all agreed that you should kill her?"

"I was working all weekend. You can ask the security guards. Craig said he would take care of the problem, and he did."

"All right. We'll see what your siblings have to add to that."

Chapter Nineteen

"I wasn't thinking clearly when I did that," Abigail insisted when Jordan sat across from her. Derek stood leaning against the wall, his expression conveying clearly that he was as fed up with the siblings' antics as everyone on this case. "I had just learned what they did, and I was too afraid to tell anyone. I was also afraid that if I didn't, the police might come for me, and see what happened." She sniffed. "I got hurt for real. I didn't want anything bad to happen to Dad. Linwood was maybe right about the money, but what they did..."

"That's not exactly what you said back at your house," Jordan reminded her.

Abby looked her straight in the eye. "You were under a lot of stress that moment, right, Detective? Maybe you don't remember correctly. Hell, I was stressed with Linwood waving that gun around. I thought he was going to shoot somebody!"

"Don't worry, Ms. Ashcroft, my memory works just fine. I remember you asked him not to get blood on the carpet. That didn't sound like you were in so much distress."

"You don't understand!" Tears were streaming down her face. "I thought if I played this really cool, I could still get out of it, and no one would know that—"

She broke off, an alarmed expression on her face. "No, it's not what you think! I didn't think they would actually kill you…"

"You didn't. A moment ago, you said you were afraid someone was going to get shot. Which one is it, Ms. Ashcroft?" Derek asked.

"I think she'll have enough time to figure that out," Jordan said, getting to her feet.

"I didn't kill anyone!" Abigail claimed. Jordan believed her, but at this point, all of them were in too deep. The only question remaining was who would take the fall.

Craig Ashcroft was still strategizing with his own lawyer. When he finally agreed to make a statement, his story was something opposite of Linwood's.

"I want to tear my hair out," Valerie said outside the interrogation room. "They are something."

"No kidding. I feel a little icky myself."

"Care for a drink after we wrap it up for today?"

"Yeah, why not?"

Derek cleared his throat, and Jordan hurried to catch up with him.

"What?"

"Nothing. I'm a little surprised, that's all."

"C'mon. You don't think…Stop it right there," she said, shaking her head. "Once we're done here, I'm going to find Ellie, head home, take a shower, and we'll hang out at the *Night Shift* for a little while. That's all."

"You're sure that's what she meant?"

"Yes, I'm sure that's what she meant."

Derek shrugged. "You must know."

"I do know. This conversation is over."

Craig Ashcroft finally admitted that one of his keys belonged to an apartment building in the city, formerly his father's, where he had taken Ms. Ryan. However, he claimed Abby and Linwood had asked him to take care of the situation.

Entering the dark apartment, Ellie gasped for breath, the memory drawing her in. She'd been trying to argue with her captor to no avail, eventually finding a small window to escape.

Given the ruthlessness of the perpetrators, she dreaded what they would find inside. She breathed a sigh of relief when they located the young woman in one of the rooms. She was scared and crying, her wrists and ankles tied together with duct tape, one strip over her mouth.

"It's over," Ellie assured her as she carefully removed the tape. "They can't hurt you anymore."

"Thank God! I thought he was just going to leave me there. Thank you." She slumped forward into Ellie's arms. Ellie let her cry for a moment, realizing that her own memory was giving way to reality and the certainty—they had won. It was perfect timing for Jordan's text message to arrive, asking to meet her at the *Night Shift* when she was ready.

When Ellie entered the bar, Jordan, Kate, Casey and Derek were already there. The latter sat at a table, while Jordan was standing at the bar, talking to the A.D.A. Ellie guessed Esposito owed Jordan an apology for not believing in her theory that Aleja Santos had been framed. They were both having a beer. After the scene she'd just left, no matter how victorious, Ellie felt like something stronger. Not for the wrong reasons.

She ordered a Martini, then went over to them and clinked her glass lightly against Jordan's bottle. "Congratulations, Detective."

"Oh, I earned them. I went through a whole day with no one trying to sue me. Instead, they're all going to go away, and Aleja's name is cleared."

"Sounds like a reason to celebrate."

Ellie assumed the A.D.A. would make her retreat, but she remained standing in the same spot, looking amused.

"You guys still have some business to take care of?"

"No." Esposito chuckled. "No more business. Thanks for your time, Jordan."

"What was that all about?" Ellie asked when Jordan followed her to their friends' table.

"Nothing. Like you said, this was a big deal."

Ellie waited, but Jordan didn't elaborate.

"You worked together before, right?" She had heard that Esposito had returned to her old job after three years out of town.

"A few times, yes," Jordan said. "Let's forget about work for a bit. That getaway you were talking about? Let's do it soon."

"Sure."

Ellie pulled herself a chair, realizing that the A.D.A. was still watching them from her spot at the bar. Perhaps she was wondering about all the changes that had taken place in her absence.

"Are you nervous about meeting Kathryn? I could still come."

"No, thank you." Jordan finished her bottle, setting it down on the table with an audible sound. "I'll call you when we're done."

Jordan couldn't believe that she had actually set this date—or that she had told Ellie not to come. Both seemed like a bad idea now that she had cleaned her house compulsively in the past hours, resisted the urge to crack open the vodka bottle she knew was in the cabinet, and now had nothing left to do but wait.

There had been no further message from Kathryn, but that didn't mean she hadn't changed her mind or wouldn't simply forget. Jordan didn't remember a time when she'd been able to count on her. It was hard to believe that this time might be different—even harder to figure out what it would mean.

At five o' clock sharp she jumped to her feet when she heard the sound of a car, but it passed by her house. 5:05. 5:10. Why should she expect anything else?

At 5:25, the doorbell rang.

"I'm so sorry." Kathryn said. She sounded out of breath. "I didn't find it right away. I went a few streets too far, so I had to go all the way back and then—"

"It's all right. Come on in."

Was this what it would boil down to? Excuses?

Kathryn followed her into the living room, taking in the surroundings with interest.

"You have a nice place," she said. "A bit far out of town, but it's beautiful."

"Thanks." Jordan didn't think Kathryn would be interested in knowing what history she had with this house, and that most of the furniture was from the former owner. "You want coffee? I made some."

"I'll have some. Thank you."

At least, that gave her something to do. Now that the moment had arrived, Jordan found it rather anti-climactic. The revelations about her biological father had stirred up a lot of emotions and uncomfortable truths, but the fact remained, she didn't know these people all that well, except from vague memories—Kathryn, Jim Larson, TJ Pratt.

She filled two cups and set them on the table. "You wanted to talk. I have to admit I'm still not sure what about exactly, but here's your chance. Talk."

Jordan hadn't missed Kathryn flinch.

"First, I want to say, whatever you might have been made to believe, I'm really proud of you, and the life you built for yourself."

"That's good to hear..." Until she reminded herself where this was coming from, and that put those words into context. "You didn't send me all those texts just to tell me that."

"No. Jordan, I want to be honest with you. I'm just still not sure how much either of us can handle."

"It's not a pretty story. I know that already."

"I know that there are some things that can't be undone, but...I want to be in your life."

"Why? You don't know me."

"You saved my life. And I know you said it's your job. I understand that. For me, it meant more. It meant I was given a chance I didn't even know I could have, to get to know you better."

So far, it was everything Jordan had expected and feared. It could only get worse.

"It took you a long time to come to that conclusion. Why not a year, or five after I'd been living with a foster family? It didn't occur to you then, that you might want to get to know me better? Oh wait. You had other things to do, like figure out where to get the dope for the next party."

She took a deep breath, uncomfortable with her own words. She understood addiction on an intellectual level. Neither

Kathryn nor Jim had been mature enough to be a parent, and there was no doubt that living with Jack and Pauline had changed her life to the better instantly. All of which were reasons why she couldn't go easy on Kathryn right now. It would have been so easy to just leave it alone.

"Yes, that was pretty much my life back then, but I swear, it's not like that anymore. I never forgot about you, I never stopped wondering. I just knew you'd be better off anywhere else than with us, and I wanted you to have that chance at a future—so you wouldn't end up the way I did. I decided to let you go because I loved you. I still do, and I hope you'll give me a chance."

This was the reason she had asked Dr. Burns to weigh in, out of fear that the truth she'd held on to for so long might be ripped from her. As long as she was still angry, that truth held.

"Just like that? You're asking a lot."

"Not just like that, I promise. If we could meet every once in a while, talk. You'd see I am different from the person you remember."

"Remember?" Jordan laughed bitterly. "You were barely present. Physically, yes, but that wasn't much of a help. Let's talk about the person I remember. How did we end up in this place anyway? You weren't pregnant with me when you married Jim."

Kathryn looked like somebody readying themselves for a blow. This was all wrong, an alternate world. She would not be tricked into sympathy. People made hard choices everyday without producing casualties along the way.

"No, I wasn't, but I was pregnant. I lost the baby—late, and I got...depressed, I guess. That's when TJ and a few other people moved into the neighborhood. Neither Jim nor I really knew how to deal with the situation, and we couldn't ask our parents for help either. The new neighbors brought lots of drugs. I was drinking on a regular basis by then, and everything else was only a matter of time. I thought it would help with the pain, but it only masked it for a while."

Jordan wasn't sure what to say, unsure whether this had been a terrible mistake. She didn't feel much in control now.

"I'm sorry about the baby," she said.

"Thank you. I didn't tell you this to make you feel bad though."

Too late.

"What happened with TJ?" From the moment the truth came out, Jordan hadn't given this question much thought, a puzzle she had forced herself to stay away from.

Kathryn held her gaze, and Jordan was startled to see her eyes well up with tears.

"Jim wasn't home one night, and I went to his trailer. There were other people there. We had a few beers, and the next thing I knew we were doing shots. One of the girls had cocaine."

"Oh God." She didn't even realize she'd spoken those words out loud.

"TJ, I know he's bad, but we were so much younger, and he could be...charming, I guess. I actually don't remember all that much, but at some point, Jim came to get me. We just went on as usual, but I think he must have suspected."

"Why didn't you give me up for adoption right away? Why wait twelve years until the police knocked on the door?"

"I thought I could do it. I'm so sorry, I really thought that time everything would be different."

"Excuse me for a moment," Jordan said. "I'll be right back."

Excuses and distractions she could handle, and even now she wasn't entirely certain Kathryn was telling her the whole truth. However, being confronted with her pain that felt raw and genuine, was more frightening than she'd ever imagined.

She had seen what TJ Pratt was capable of. She wouldn't put it past him to take advantage of a young neighbor, thirty-something years ago.

Ellie picked up right away. The relief was making her knees weak.

"Hey," Jordan said, leaning against the counter.

"Hey, how's it going? Is she gone?"

"No. Could you please come?"

"Is something wrong? I'll leave right away. If you want me to talk to her, I will. She's not blaming you for any of this, right? In that case, I'm ready to give her a piece of my mind."

"No, it's not like that. I'd just like to see you."

"You'll see me in a few minutes, I promise," Ellie whispered. "I love you."

"I love you too," Jordan said, but Ellie was already gone. She went back to the living room where Kathryn hadn't moved. "When you said you don't remember..."

"I wanted to get drunk, high, have sex with somebody."

This time, it was Jordan who flinched at her birthmother's brutal honesty. "Does that make a difference to you? If he had raped me, would it be easier for you to forgive me?"

"That's a big word. TJ Pratt hurt a lot of people. He killed a young officer who was a colleague of mine, and another almost died. You want the truth? I'm glad he didn't rape you. I'm just not ready to forgive you. I'm sorry if you expected that coming here."

Kathryn was silent for a moment, letting every word sink in.

"I respect that," she finally said. "I have to. Can I see you again? I'd love to make most of the time I have left."

"What does that mean? Did your tests come back?"

Kathryn got to her feet. "Yes, they did, and the results are...not great. I'm not terminally ill or anything, but I need to make some changes. I had hoped that being able to see you would be one of those changes."

"I lead a pretty busy life. I think...give me some time, okay? A few weeks. I'll call you."

Control.

"That would be wonderful. Thank you for seeing me. It means a lot."

Kathryn stepped forward, and because she had no room to escape, Jordan let herself be embraced. She didn't hug her back, though, and sensing her reserve, Kathryn took a step backwards.

"I know it's a lot to think about. Please know that you've been on my mind, and the beautiful life your parents were going to give you. Back in those days, we didn't always think of the police as our friends."

"I wonder why," Jordan muttered.

"You saved me. You have become an extraordinary woman. If I had to do it all over again, give you up to make that happen, I'm sorry, I would."

Abruptly, she turned on her heels and left before Jordan could react in any way.

What if you had tried harder instead?

She sank onto the armchair, leaning forward. The truth was, Jordan knew all about what it was like to try as hard as you could and still fail. She had picked up the pieces. That made all the difference in the world. Didn't it?

Chapter Twenty

E llie was in her arms a split-second after she opened the door to her. It felt so good that it took Jordan a while to step back and take in her appearance. Her short dress and boots were clearly for a night out. Jordan wasn't sure she was up to it, but it might be better than trying to analyze Kathryn's story and what it meant for her, right now. She would have liked to stop thinking altogether for a while.

Something else was new.

"You changed your hair back."

"Yes, I did. I thought you could use something to cheer you up today..." Ellie nervously tugged on a strand of her newly auburn colored hair. "I hope it's a good surprise."

"You're beautiful. I mean, of course you were beautiful before, but this is actually your natural color."

A smile lit up Ellie's face. "You would know."

"I would. And it's totally working, thank you. But you didn't get into this outfit so I could take if off of you right away—or did you?"

"Later," Ellie said, her cheeks reddening. "For now, there's somewhere I wanted to go with you...and I thought we could have dinner in town after. Kate is staying at Derek's for the weekend, so we have the place to ourselves again. If you want to talk..."

"Just let me change and we can leave."

Kathryn was right about one thing. Jordan had been given the chance to become someone other than a carbon copy of her birthmother, repeating the same mistakes. All the times she'd struggled, with being faithful, with drinking too much, it was behind her now. If she left that in the past, she could do the same with her anger, her accusations, even if they were righteous. She had a different life now, with a woman who loved her, and a job for which she still had the right instincts. Time to move on.

⁂

Ellie had known it would be a good idea to take Jordan to see Darla. While she hadn't completely made up her mind about Kathryn, she was and would always be partial to Jordan.

Darla looked a lot better than the last time she'd seen her. She was allowed to get up and see her son, so Jordan and Ellie joined her.

"Aren't you proud of me? This was my toughest assignment so far," she joked.

"How is he? Did you name him yet?"

"He's gaining weight, so that's good. I actually did come up with a name. It's Jordan Avery Pierson."

"You're kidding me."

"I'm not. For all those donuts and specialty coffees you bought me, you deserve it. Now I am kidding. But you know why."

"I'm honored." Jordan carefully embraced the younger woman. "You'll be a great mom."

Ellie couldn't help smiling, glad Jordan had found those words. "Anything you need, you know where to find us," she said. "Let us know when you can go home. One of us can give you a ride."

"Thank you so much. This little guy will have to stay a little bit longer, but I know he'll be okay. He's a fighter."

"I can see where he got it from," Jordan said.

Ellie had made reservations earlier, just in case, so they could get a quiet table at one of their favorite restaurants in the city.

"I really don't want to talk about me all the time. Or Kathryn. It is what it is, and she seems to be honest wanting to make amends. I guess I can live with that. What about you?"

"I can live with that too," Ellie said quickly.

"That's not what I meant."

"I didn't feel like I was going to have a panic attack when we opened up that apartment. So that's good."

"It is."

"Truth be told, I was so busy I didn't have time to think about it much. I still have...nightmares sometimes." She stopped while the waiter filled their glasses and continued when he had left. "I know you do too. It will become less over time. I'm going to live my life. Be with you. Take the detective's exam eventually. They can't take that away from us."

"Sounds good to me." Jordan raised her glass, and Ellie touched hers against it with a soft clink. "You were always the one with the plan. I admired that from the moment I met you."

"I'm not sure if my plans were always good." Ellie laughed softly. "But thank you. I admire you, period. You think you could stand having to work with me every day? If I moved upstairs?"

"Why not? We already work well together."

"Yeah. Even if Bristol thinks I'm spending a bit too much time with you guys. Don't worry." She held up a hand at Jordan's alarmed expression. "He was nice about it when he told me, but that made me think I need to get back to studying. When it's time, I want no delays."

"See. Plans." Jordan took her hand, holding it in hers gently.

"Speaking of which," Ellie said, "I know we were kind of laughing when Pauline mentioned it, but I was wondering if you've been thinking about kids...lately."

"Plural? I have thought about it, but my answer is still the same. I want you to be comfortable, take that test, do what you want to do. That's priority to me, and besides, I still fear I would be a terrible mother."

"You wouldn't be, but there's no rush. I just bring it up so you know you can talk to me about these things...planning the future. Because you're stuck with me."

"That's fine. Because there's nowhere else I'd rather be."

Ellie couldn't help smiling at that, thinking how far they'd come. She still had to ask. "How bad was it?"

"Not as bad as I expected. Worse in some respect," Jordan said honestly. "I'm not twelve anymore, and I realize there's a limit as to how we can make things better for each other. Anger takes a lot of energy. My focus is elsewhere now."

"That's a good thing."

As far as Ellie was concerned, it was only the beginning of good things to come. It was true that she usually had a plan. It was coming true, even if they still lived in separate apartments.

❧

They spent a quiet weekend at Jordan's house. Having coffee on the deck, listening to the sounds of birds, Ellie had to admit there was some advantage to this more remote neighborhood. It was just hard to get over the fact, still, that the man who had sold it to her was a convicted serial killer. It was puzzling to Ellie that Jordan could disregard it considering the harm Darby had done her—but it worked for her. The space was beautiful without a doubt, but it was also a half hour drive into the city without traffic, something inconvenient when having to get to work on a Monday morning.

At roll call, Ellie was still too content with the course of the weekend and her life in general to react to Chris Atwood whistling as she walked by, whispering something to his buddy. She sat down next to Kate whose eyes widened when she saw Ellie.

"What?"

"He's a jerk, but I'd whistle too if I could. You look great. So, you're not a natural blonde after all."

"Great. I'm going to hear variations of this all day, I assume."

"Prepare for it. Looks great on you."

Sergeant Bristol walked in, and Ellie could swear there was a flash of surprise on his face when he saw her. She barely suppressed a sigh.

⁂

No matter how good your life could get, sometimes it just—stank. Jordan tried not to breathe too deeply as she and Derek were standing at the landfill site where workers had reported a body minutes ago.

"What a way to start off the week, huh?"

The woman was face-down, in her twenties maybe, wearing a long dress over a blouse, her hair in a braid that was now disheveled, dirt everywhere. It looked more like a costume than what a woman her age might wear on a daily basis, but it was hard to tell. What Jordan found most disturbing was that with the dress riding up, she couldn't see any underwear.

The scene was already busy, officers taping off the area. The medical examiner's team had arrived.

Jordan watched as they carefully moved the body around. There was less damage to the woman's face than she'd feared.

"Oh God," she heard the soft whisper behind her.

Turning around to find Kate McCarthy's face an alarming color, she said, "If you're going to be sick, I understand, but please, go outside the tape, okay?"

Kate shook her head, still ghostly pale. "I'm feeling pretty sick right now, but that's not it. The woman...it's Jennifer Beaumont."

Ellie came up behind her, laying a hand on her shoulder.

"I have to tell her mother," Kate said, close to tears.

"No, you don't have to. This is now on a completely different scale. We'll take care of it." It was without a doubt the worst part of the job, but Kate had been personally invested. Jordan didn't think this should be any more traumatic on her than it needed to be.

"You don't understand. I have to."

"Kate. Jordan is right."

Ignoring Derek's words, and anyone else's, Kate turned and walked away. Ellie hurried to catch up with her.

Jordan crouched next to the body of the young woman who had been on her way to visit her mother but then disappeared after being seen with the man Rhonda Marks had briefly dated.

They'd had to let him go, but this changed everything.

Raphael Deane would have to answer many more questions.

About the Author

B arbara Winkes writes sapphic crime drama and Christ-mas romance. She loves writing characters who get the job done, whether it's stopping a predator or saving cherished traditions—while still making time for love. She lives with her wife in Quebec City.

barbarawinkes.com

Also by Barbara Winkes

The Crossing Lines Trilogy
Undercover
Redemption
Vengeance

The Connected Series
Promised to the Queen
Drawn to the Enemy
Tempted by the Protector

Kelli & Merin Romantic Suspense
Thunder
Rain

Standalone
The Amnesia Project